Dumarest longed for an emptier sky. One illuminated by the swollen bulk of a silver moon blotched in the likeness of a skull. Of constellations which formed patterns holding the likeness of men and beasts, women and creatures of the sea. The signposts of Earth—wherever that might be.

A world lost in distance and time so that even its name had become a legend. But one now so close, so very close!

Dumarest looked up again at the sky and felt again the surge he had known in the market. One born of the sudden realization that, at last, his search could be over. That the answer he had hunted for so long was at hand.

Melome could find it.

She *had* to find it!

MELOME

E. C. Tubb

DAW BOOKS, INC.
DONALD A. WOLLHEIM, PUBLISHER

1633 Broadway, New York, NY 10019

Dedication

To ROY and DAPHNE MORTIMER

First Printing, June 1983

1 2 3 4 5 6 7 8 9

 DAW TRADEMARK REGISTERED
U.S. PAT. OFF. MARCA
REGISTRADA. HECHO EN U.S.A.

PRINTED IN U.S.A.

CHAPTER ONE

———————

Dumarest heard the scream of a tortured child and turned, eyes searching, relaxing as it came again and he recognized the source. A hundred yards to his right, raised high above the decorated surface of the boulevard, a painted crone lolled on a gilded throne standing on a platform of massive timbers supported by a dozen stalwarts. They, in turn, stood on another platform, larger, borne by twice their number. Overseers lashed them on with whips which left carmine streaks on naked, sweating flesh.

A show as false as the screams; a mature beauty lay beneath the masking paint and the massive timbers were thin cladding over buoyant rafts. Props for the actors demonstrating their skills; the grimaces, the fatigue, the grunts of pain. The whips were thin tubes containing dye but the men wielding them were clever as was the woman with her screams.

She shrieked again as Dumarest watched, the cry now accompanied by the clash of beaten metal, the harsh tintinnabulation prolonged by the chime of tiny bells. A score of girls ran from the shelter of the lower platform, weaving among the spectators, one coming to a halt before Dumarest.

"My lord—do I please you?" She was young, lithe, radiating unabashed femininity. Bells circled her ankles and wrists, more caressing the column of her throat, the narrow cincture of her waist. The long skirt, slit to the hip, displayed naked, slender legs, the hint of unclothed loins. Paint accentuated the luster of her eyes, the soft fullness of her lips. Curled hair the color of gold held the glint of metal and gems. "My lord?"

A girl demanding his attention as the screams of the crone had caught it. The girl smiled as he nodded, chiming as she moved, the bound of unfettered breasts an enticing invitation.

"You are gracious, my lord." Her eyes were frank in their appraisal. "It would pleasure me to serve you. At the circus of Chen Wei. A spectacle of marvels culled from a thousand worlds. Things which will amaze you, amuse you, puzzle you, fill you with rapture. A feast for the eye and ear and mind and one not to be missed. The circus of Chen Wei. And, if you should be in a mind for dalliance—" Her face became lewd with unspoken promise. "My name is Helga. Ask for Helga."

A smile and she was gone leaving nothing but the scent of perfume and the fading tinkle of bells. Things which belonged on Baatz, and Dumarest took a deep breath as he looked at the sky, the hills, the boulevard on which he stood. It ran arrow-straight from the landing field to the market, the surface tesselated in abstract designs, curlicues, broken rainbows. Triple-tiered buildings edged the wide road, dwellings, shops, businesses, the verandas gaudy with bright hangings, the roofs with bloated lanterns. On the flanking hills the mansions of the rich and influential rested like a scatter of gems.

A good world, one of balm, of warmth and gentle breezes, of golden sunlight and rounded hills. A place of tranquility; the exudations of massed vegetation filling the air with subtle vapors which took the edge off violence and aggression and induced a tolerant lethargy.

A danger he recognized but could do nothing about and it was good to relax, to enjoy the sun, to become one with the crowd. To feel wide expanses around him instead of the cramping confines of a hull. And Baatz, with its transient population, was as good a place as any for him to be.

But caution remained and before he moved on, Dumarest made sure that none had lingered for no apparent reason, that he wasn't the object of covert interest. All seemed innocuous, most had followed the spectacle advertising the circus, others were intent on their own affairs, the rest headed toward the market, the sights, sounds and smells it contained.

"My lord!" A woman dressed in the barbaric apparel of a warrior-amazon gestured with an imperious arm. "Fine weaves from Kirek, strands as tough as steel and as soft as silk—nothing can beat spider-webs for utility. I have fifteen bales of it—you offer?''

A scowl marred the mannish face as Dumarest moved on, the voice yielding to another.

"High quality grain proof against bacterial molds and virus infestation. Strains from the biolabs of Lengue and Femarre. Fifteen kobolds a measure. Buy! Buy! Buy!"

A man stepped forward, another catching at his arm.

"Wait, Krasse. It could be cheaper deeper in the market."

"And less trustworthy. I've dealt with Chamile before and I don't trust you among the stalls. Best to buy here and now and get back to the farm before you've spent all we have."

Brothers or partners—they fell behind as Dumarest moved on. Booths and stalls stretched on all sides, some bearing a profusion of items, some only a few. Many held examples of goods housed in the holds of the vessels which had carried them. Others showed goods yet to arrive or dealt in future harvests, the samples on display examples of earlier yields. Stalls bearing gems of price were set next to those heaped with the cheap glitter of rubbish.

Businessmen, traders, thieves, entrepreneurs—the market of Baatz catered to all.

The jangle of a bell and the echo of a gong announced an operation in progress and Dumarest halted at the booth of a transient healer. The man was old, his robe not as spotless as it could have been, but he was deft and practice had augmented his skill. The patient was seated, eyes wide, the milky orbs already anesthetized. A woman in middle age attended by a young girl who watched with horror as the needle was applied. Within seconds it had been done, the cataracts removed and the eyes bandaged. The assistant had been generous with the prophylactic spray.

"Here, my dear." The healer handed the girl a phial. "All done and nothing to worry about. Give your mother this draught as soon as you get her home."

A strong sedative with a touch of slowtime; the woman would sleep while her accelerated metabolism speeded the healing process. She would wake rested, hungry—and cured.

Another booth housed a dentist, another a dealer in charms, yet another a man who promised a cure for all the afflictions of the heart.

A fortune teller sat staring into a bowl of sand, the fine grains spurting in a random pattern of plumes.

A man swallowed flame.

A boy lay screaming on the ground, held by four men while, over his naked chest crawled the insect whose bite would cure him of the epilepsy which controlled him.

"Earl!" Evan Luftman waved from where he stood chewing at a mouthful of meat. "Enjoying the sights?"

"Just looking around."

"Baatz holds everything a man could need." Luftman wiped his mouth and looked at the skewer he held. On it fragments of meat lay beside succulent vegetables, the whole flavored with spice. "Good food, amiable women, diversions of all kinds. Going to the circus?"

"Maybe."

"They say it's good. Something special." Luftman licked at his skewer. "If those girls are anything to go by they weren't lying."

Dumarest made no comment. Luftman had been a fellow passenger on the journey to Baatz. They'd killed time over the card table and the man had talked more than he had wanted to listen. A roving entrepreneur dealing in what came to hand. A man past middle age with a face creased and blotched by the passage of time and dissipation. The meeting was one he could have done without.

"I've finished my business," said Luftman. "A quick profit, small but a man can't be too greedy. Now I'm looking for a couple of healers willing to travel to Jardis. They have a lot of eye trouble in the mines and it costs money to ship in regular doctors. Working on a profit-sharing basis I figure three months should make us all a comfortable pile."

"It could."

"It will if—" Luftman looked at his skewer then threw it aside. "I could use someone to take care of things, Earl. Muscle in case it's needed. Those miners can get awkward at times. Refuse to pay after treatment or gang up and demand a refund. You know how it can be."

"You can handle it."

"Once, yes, not now. I can't face them down, not like you could. One-fifth the profit, Earl. Maybe three months' work. A deal?"

"For a fifth?"

"Make it a quarter. An even share, Earl, you, me, the two healers—after expenses, naturally."

Which would be high. Dumarest said, "When are you leaving?"

"On the *Yegor*. It leaves at midnight. Be on the field an hour before then."

A rendezvous Dumarest hadn't made and wouldn't keep. Luftman's scheme held little appeal, and the only one to gain would be the entrepreneur himself. If he could find willing healers—even on Baatz trusting fools were rare.

On the ground the writhing boy shrieked, twisted, shrieked again as the mandibles of the insect fed healing venom into his blood. A convulsive heave and he slumped. Head tilted to one side, lips parted to bare the teeth, the rod clamped between them.

In the comparative silence Dumarest heard the rattle of clashing ceramics, the whine of a female voice broken by the brittle sound.

". . . gather to hear . . . *clash* . . . the ancient . . . *clash*. . . songs of . . . *clash* . . . *clash* . . . Terra."

Terra?

Earth!

She stood in a ragged circle of semi-curious spectators, a girl little more than a child with long, straggling hair the color of sun-bleached bone, eyes like bruises, a mouth of bloodless lips and down-curved corners. Her skin matched the color of her hair, pale, waxen. The limbs were brittle appendages, nails of hands and naked feet rimmed with dirt. A frayed skirt hugged boyish loins and a halter shielded nascent breasts. Her waist, bare, was circled by a metal belt from which hung strands ending in spooled grips.

"Melome!" The woman standing beside her rattled her cluster of ceramic shards. "Who dares to test her powers? What man is brave enough to yield to her skill and taste the acid burn of remembered fears? What woman has the strength to shred the veil hiding her secret dreads?" Again the brittle chiming. "You, sir? You? You, my lady?"

A grifter and a good one; gaining attention, building a pitch, selecting the marks even as she spoke. A boy, blushing, looked at the spooled grip she thrust into his hand. A woman frowned as she was given another. Two men, grinning, took their places.

"Guaranteed entertainment for a mere five kobolds and your money back if dissatisfied. You, sir? Here, my lord!"

Dumarest felt the spool thrust into his hand and held it as he stared at the woman. She was no longer young, raddled beneath her paint, the body shapeless, the eyes hard.

He said, "You spoke of Terra."

"Terror, my lord? Aye, that and more for those with the courage to face it. Here you will find the ancient and dire songs of fear and hate and abject terror. Threnodies to chill the blood and numb the mind. A unique experience and one not to be missed. You there, sir! And you!"

A mistake, one born of noise and confusion, and natural enough to make. The twist of a vowel—yet for a moment there had been hope. The hope died as Dumarest looked again at the girl, the older woman, the two men squatting to one side. Ragged, both old, one with a drum, the other holding a pipe. Its wail rose as the woman returned to halt before him.

"The last place, my lord. Take it and we can begin."

A market-spectacle, born of illusion and the circumstance of the moment; it could be little more than that. But curiosity remained, why the belt, the connecting strands? How did the woman hope to prevent those who had not paid from enjoying what she had to offer?

"My lord!" The woman smiled as she took his money and handed him the spool. "Be seated. All be seated and let the entertainment commence!"

The spool was spring-loaded, the strand remaining taut as Dumarest sat on the ground, forming a connection between his hand and the belt the girl wore against her naked flesh. Connections repeated by all who had paid to join the circle. Like a spider in the center of a shimmering web the girl stood, motionless.

The tap of the drum joined the wail of the pipe, a throbbing, monotonous beat which seemed too loud for the instrument, as the wail of the pipe seemed too loud, the sudden hush drowning normal sounds too strong. A moment in which his eyes followed the glinting strand, moved to others, returned to his own and then, without warning, the girl began to sing.

A song without words.

One which filled the universe.

Dumarest had known the Ghenka-art which took vocal sound and used it to gain a hypnotic compulsion in which the mind was opened to flower in a profusion of mental images. He had heard the song of a living jewel and would never forget the awesome tonal effects of Gath. But this diminished them all.

A song—no, a dirge—no, a paen—no, a threnody, a lilting cadence, a sobbing, sighing, heart-wrenching murmur which created sympathetic vibrations from the thin strands so that they, too, sang in metallic harmony. A quivering which seemed to cloud the air and mask the slender figure in writhing strands of light and darkness. A chiaroscuro which blurred and changed to become a face snarling in anger.

One Dumarest had seen before.

It swelled to fill his vision, small details becoming plain; the eyes with their yellow tinge, the thinned, cracked lips, the nostrils rimmed with mucous, the ears tufted with hair. The face of a man who intended to kill.

One without a name on a world far distant in a time long forgotten, but Dumarest felt again the shock he had known then; the sudden realization that he had been duped and what he'd thought was a practice bout was the stage for his public butchery.

The shock and the terror. The fear and pain as edged steel cut a channel across his torso and sent blood to stain the floor of the ring. The lights, the weight of his own blade, the ring of avid faces but, above all, the terror of being maimed, crippled, blinded, turned into a mewling, helpless thing.

The face promised it all, the man, the knife he held, the profession he was in. A trained and savage killer amusing himself with an inexperienced boy. One who had no choice but to learn fast.

To move, to dodge and weave, to cut and slash and rip and stab and to find speed and use it. To be fast . . . fast . . . fast . . .

But the terror remained and would always remain if only as a whispering echo in the dim regions of his psyche. A weakness which strengthened his iron determination to survive.

He blinked, aware of the spool in his hand, the sweat dewing his face. To one side a man rocked, wailing, tears falling over his cheeks. Another shuddered, quivering. A woman appealed to invisible ghosts.

"No! Dear God, please! Please!"

Facing Dumarest the young boy looked sick, one of the two laughing men stared blankly at his clenched hand, his companion had a blood-smeared chin from a bitten lip.

Only the girl seemed unchanged. She stood as Dumarest remembered, head lowered a little, eyes blank, hands limp at her sides. A sensitive, he guessed. Someone with an unusual attribute which she barely recognized and had paid for with physical penalties; weakness, poor development, lethargy, stunted growth.

"Wine, my lord?" The woman was beside him, a tray of brimming cups in her hand. "A kobold only."

A high price for weak liquor but of them all he was the only one to refuse. And none had asked for a return of their money.

Dumarest heard the clash of the ceramics again as he moved away. Unnecessary advertising; the spectacle of how the song had affected the initial group would be attraction enough but, he guessed, the girl would need a little time between performances to gain strength. Even a normal singer would need that.

He heard the wail of the pipe as he bought wine at a booth, sipping it slowly, hearing the pulse of the drum merge with the wail, the peculiar distortion which seemed to muffle the sound. Of the song he heard nothing.

"Clever." The vendor wiped his hands on his apron as he nodded toward the place where the girl operated. "She sings but unless you're in contact you hear nothing. An electronic barrier, I guess."

"Have you tried her?"

"No. I've no love for terror and the sight of those who've tasted it is enough to tell me I'm right. Still, I can't complain, it's good for business if nothing else."

Dumarest looked at his glass. "I guess it is. Has she been here long?"

"I wouldn't know. I only relieved my partner a week ago. She was here then."

"Alone or—"

"With the woman. Kamala's hard in her way but I guess she's fair enough. Someone has to look after the girl and Kamala knows how to take care of a valuable property. She could do worse." The vendor wiped his hands again. "More wine?"

A hint, even on Baatz information had to be paid for, but the wine was good and helped to dispel the chill induced by remembered terror. Or had it been simply remembered?

Dumarest recalled the face, the details he had noted, the pain he had experienced. Real pain as the lights had been real, the knife in his hand, the avid faces. A montage of isolated incidents? A possibility but he doubted it; somehow the song had opened a door in his mind. Touching a node and triggering a total recall of an emotion-loaded incident. One unique to himself.

To one side a juggler wafted a dozen glittering balls into the air, keeping them spinning as he danced on a floor spiked with points. Next to him a girl undulated in an erotic rhythm while beyond a man with a stall loaded with hoes frowned his displeasure. Dumarest ignored them all, seeing nothing but the trembling of his own hand, feeling nothing but the surge which warmed his blood. Luck—it had always been with him, but now it seemed overwhelming.

The girl, Melome, could give him far more than a song.

Kalama said, "My lord, it is not wise. You should not—"

"Here!" Dumarest cut her short, thrusting money into her hand, snatching a spool from the fingers of another. "Let us begin."

Impatience rode him, displayed in the small act of violence which made him the center of attention, a thing he ignored as he sat, looking at the metallic strand, the girl standing within her web. One who seemed to blur as the throb of the drum merged with the wail of the pipe, to become a focus, an instrument he sought to use.

A key to explore the past.

He concentrated, narrowing possibilities, honing his mind to a single thought and then the terror came, the fear, the sick and hollow feeling in his guts.

The wind like a razor on his cheeks.

The cold, the hunger, the feel of the gritty soil, the desperation. The conviction that he would die.

Before him the bulk of a ship rested in a strange and enigmatic beauty. The first he had seen but, young though he was, he knew it held the warmth and food he needed if he hoped to survive. He edged toward it, a child older than his years, one who had killed and was ready to kill again. The crew were careless, not seeing the small shape which darted from point to point, freezing, moving again with frenzied urgency.

To reach the port, to dive inside, to find a nook in which to crouch. To wait, dozing, as the unaccustomed warmth gave a false security, to jerk to awareness, to doze again.

To wake heart pounding with terror at the touch of a hand, the sight of a startled face, another which scowled.

"By God, look what we have here! A damned stowaway."

"A kid."

"Still a stowaway. That's what you are, boy. Know how we treat scum like you? Into the lock and out, that's how. Dumped into the void. Your eyes'll pop out and your lungs will become balloons frothing from your mouth. You'll look like raw meat—ruined but still alive. A hell of a way to go."

"Don't make a meal of it." The other man was uneasy. "You don't have to gloat. Anyway, it's up to the skipper to decide."

The captain was old, his face lined, graced with tufted eyebrows, his nose pinched and set above a firm mouth.

"How old are you, boy? Ten? Eleven?"

"Yes, sir."

"Yes, what? Eleven?"

"Twelve, I think, sir. I'm not sure." The face before him blurred, jarred to clear focus. "Sir?"

"I could dump you but I won't. You can ride with us, working your passage. A hard life but better than what you've known." Again the blurring. "Food, warmth, security—but you'll earn it all."

"Sir? I—sir?"

But the face had gone and he looked at a glittering strand and the girl to which it led while, from the circle of which he was a part, came the groans and wails of those who had tasted an evil fruit.

"Wine?"

Kamala was beside him with her tray of beakers and Dumarest bought and sipped while retaining his place. The moment had been too short; memories revived and speeded by subjective time so that he had lived an hour, more, in a few minutes. Or was it simply that? Did the moment of terror, once experienced, form the whole of the incident?

He had been a boy again, back home on Earth, and only the ship and the captain's kindness had saved him from death. But there had been other moments of terror; times when through ignorance he had known the fear of a trapped animal. One augmented by the threats of sadistic members of the crew who had taken a perverse delight in relating stories of dreadful punishments inflicted for small wrongs.

Of burnings, beating, maiming, blinding—things which his experience had told him were all too possible.

Time had negated them; the savagery he had known had no place in any civilized community, but, until he had learned, terror had been a close companion.

"My lord?" Kamala again, looking at his barely touched wine, the spool still held in his free hand. "Is something wrong?"

Dumarest realized that he alone was left of the circle. Finishing the wine, he handed the woman the empty beaker. He followed it with coins.

Kamala refused them with a shake of the head.

"No, my lord, it would not be wise. I warned you against hearing the song again so soon. Yield again to terror and—"

"I won't go mad."

"So you say and it could well be true but others have made the same boast and failed to live up to it. I want no trouble."

Dumarest said, flatly, "I've the money and I'm in position. Rattle your chimes, woman, and stop wasting time."

"No."

"You want a higher fee? Double, then. Triple. Damn it, name your price!"

"No!" She backed from the anger blazing in his eyes, one hand lifting, steadying, the massive ring she wore on the index finger glowing with a metallic sheen. A weapon he recognized. "Baatz is a peaceful world," she said. "But a woman would be a fool to be without protection on any world and, my lord, I am not a fool. It would be best for you to leave now."

Advice he was reluctant to take. Pressed, he could negate the threat of the weapon, moving before she could discharge its darts, reaching her, twisting hand and wrist so as to obtain the ring. But if he used his superior speed and strength he would ensure her enmity. It was better to master his impatience.

"My lady, I must apologize." A smile replaced the anger which had frightened her. "I mean no harm and want no trouble. It was just that—well, I'm sure you understand."

"You're holding the spool."

"Is that bad?"

"Release it."

"Of course." He let it fall and watched as it moved toward the girl, the reel climbing the strand to hang at her belt. "I would like to talk business." He added, as she frowned, "At least let me make the offer."

"Melome sings no more today." Kalama was adamant. "She is tired and soon it will be dark. Not even for two hundred kobolds will she sing."

Twice what she would earn in a session; a score of spools hung at her waist. But if he should offer more? Dumarest decided against it; as Kalama had said, the girl was tired and the sky held the hint of coming darkness. In the softening light Melome stood like a broken animal, one which had been ridden too hard and too far. The lowered face was ghastly in its pallor, the bruised eyes ugly smears.

He said, "I understand, but I want her to sing for me again. A private performance—it can be arranged?"

"Perhaps." The lifted hand wavered a little, fell as, again, he smiled. "You want to buy her?"

"Hire her."

"For an hour, a day, a week?" Her lips twisted in a cynical lewdness. "It will not be as you hope. Those in the grip of terror make poor lovers."

Dumarest said, patiently, "I want her to sing and that is all. To sing to me alone and to keep on singing if I ask. Once may be enough. One song—two hundred and fifty?"

"Not tonight," she said quickly. "One song, you said. If you should want more?"

"Five hundred for as many as I want. For a session to end when I say so."

"Five songs only—and she stops if the strain is too great." Again her mouth displayed cynical distrust. "You have no objection to me being present?"

"None."

"And my instrumentalists?"

"I want her to sing," said Dumarest. "Nothing else." He jingled coins from one hand to the other. "Here is fifty as proof of my good faith. At dawn?"

"At midday. Be at the house of the Broken—no, better we visit you." Kalama nodded as he gave the address of the room he'd hired. "At noon then, my lord. Be patient in your waiting."

Patient but not foolish and it was dark by the time Dumarest left the market. Even at night the place was still alive; lamps burning with swaths of red and gold, blue and umber, the scent of cooking meats and vegetables hanging in the air together with writhing plumes of incense, sparks from torches, beams from shimmering orbs of kaleidoscopic hues. Mundane trading had ended, the vendors of hoes and seeds and domestic items giving way to others who filled the night with a different allure. Drummers and pipers together with dancers, the thin whine of strings, the drone of flutes. Gamblers who called from tables set with cards, dice, hollow shells. Women with snakes, spiders, crawling beetles. The tellers of fortunes and artists who created glowing picture on living skin.

Men who fought with knives.

Practice blades; edges and points shielded and capable of dealing little more than bruises and scratches. And the bouts lacked the savage intensity normal to any good fighter—the magic of Baatz had robbed them of serious intent so that the crowd laughed at bad play instead of jeering and the loser accepted defeat with a grin and a shrug.

"Sir!" The promotor had spotted Dumarest, noted his height, his stance, the hilt of the knife riding above his right boot. "A bout, sir? You look like a man used to the arena. A little harmless sport to entertain lovers of the art. A demonstration of skill, the winner decided by popular acclaim. No?" His voice held a philosophical shrug. "Then how about you, sir? Or you?"

Dumarest walked on. Ahead the lights of the boulevard matched those of the stars now illuminating the sky; clusters of vibrant colors, sheets and curtains of luminescence, nebulae like smoke. Too many stars and he longed for an emptier sky. One illuminated by the swollen bulk of a silver moon blotched in the likeness of a skull. Of constellations which formed patterns holding the likeness of men and beasts, women and creatures of the sea. The signposts of Earth—wherever that might be.

A world lost in distance and time so that even its name had become a legend.

But one now so close. So very close!

Dumarest halted, leaning against a wall, looking up at the sky and feeling again the surge he had known in the market. One born of the sudden realization that, at last, his search could be over. That the answer he had hunted for so long was at hand.

Melome could find it.

She *had* to find it!

Waking that moment in the past when, as a child, he had stood in the captain's cabin and stared uncomprehendingly at the volume on the desk. A book which had meant nothing at the time and he had turned from it in sudden terror as footsteps came from the passage. If discovered, he could be accused of prying or stealing, be beaten, maimed, tormented—his sadistic mentors had taught him well.

But that terror, stimulated by the song, would bring the book again before his eyes, the data it contained. All he had to do was wait.

Then noon passed and the girl did not appear and when he went searching he learned she had been sold to the circus of Chen Wei.

CHAPTER TWO

The man was a grotesquerie; a thing of extended limbs, massive ears, lumps, bumps, protrusions. A clown cavorting on stilts, the painted face ludicrous above a padded torso. The hair was like a brush touched with a dozen hues. The voice was like an organ.

"Why hesitate? The circus of Chen Wei waits to entertain you. See novelties, marvels, impossibilities. Wander in realms of mystic enchantment. Thrill to the impact of exotic stimuli. The chance of a lifetime. Not to be missed. Hurry, now. Hurry! Hurry! Hurry!"

A bell clanged, three acrobats spun in a confusion of sequins and satin, a woman sold tickets.

"Ten for transport and the same for initial entry. Twenty, kobolds—thank you, sir. Keep the stub for your return."

A dwarf guided Dumarest to where rafts waited in line urging him into the first where he sat on a bench next to the rail. A girl came to join him, another at her side. She was young, eager to enjoy her day, hopeful for masculine company but after one glance at his face she turned to her friend leaving Dumarest to stare at the ground below.

It fell away as the raft lifted, streaming beneath in an unbroken expanse of curled and matted vegetation dotted with delicate flowers. The afternoon sun touched them, turned them into scraps of gold, of ruby, of smoking amber. Flecks which looked like eyes and all of them mocking.

Why had he been such a fool?

Melome had been in his hand—he should never have let her go. Never have trusted Kalama to keep their bargain. What had made him so careless? He had quested the market and gained her address, verifying it from more than one source. An elementary precaution, but why hadn't he done more? Why had he been content to wait until it was too late? The woman had cheated him but the money was nothing; he would willingly give ten times as much to correct his stupidity.

"Mister?" The girl at his side pointed over the rail. "Is that the circus?"

"No—I don't know."

"Sorry. I thought maybe you'd been before. My friend thought you might have done. A lot of people have done. That is—" He wasn't listening and she knew it. "Sorry."

An apology Kalama would never have to make. She was gone, probably on the *Yegor*—he had seen the ship head for space wreathed in the blue cocoon of its Erhaft field. Robbing him even of revenge. Leaving Melome—his hand tightened as he thought about it. Closed in anger more against himself than Kalama. What use to blame another for his folly?

One caused by the wine or the shock of the song or the emotional impact of realizing what Melome could give him. Like a climber reaching a summit, confident of success, hurrying a little—and taking that one false step which led to destruction. Thinking more about that moment when, in the captain's cabin, he had seen the book on the desk. A journal, perhaps, or the ship's log he had brought up to date. But both would have held the details of his journeys.

Both would have held the coordinates of Earth.

"There!" The girl at his side, excited, rose as she pointed. "There it is!"

Froth cupped in a fold of the hills. Bubbles laced and striped with gaudy candy colors; vivid purples, reds, greens, blues, sickly yellows, lambent violet. Spires bearing floating pennants. Twisted towers topped with flags. Walks and slides and curving spirals. Peaked roofs graced with undulating crests.

The circus of Chen Wei.

Dumarest studied it as the raft dropped to the landing. Much of what he saw had to be mirage; illusions created with paint and fabric, using distorted perspective to give the impression of buildings and space where none existed. A spire vanished as he looked at it, became a blur of lines and blotches, became a spire again as he turned his head. An optical illusion repeated on all sides as cubes, stairs, landings shifted and took on other dimensions.

"Welcome to the circus!" A clown like a ball bounded toward them, another on stilts stood, beaming, as a man with a crested headpiece took their tickets, tore them, returned the stubs. "Enter and enjoy! Hurry! Hurry! Hurry!"

Entry was through a giant, laughing mouth, the passage forming the throat set with a series of spongy rollers; air traps which kept the internal pressure high. Dumarest pushed his way through them to emerge in a playground filled with seats, stalls, niches holding bizarre statues. A fountain shone with shifting luminescence while filling the air with crystalline merriment. Sideshows ran to either side, barkers shouting their spiel. A place of fun and games and assorted entertainment.

All that the initial entry ticket would buy.

Dumarest checked the sideshows and moved on, paying for admission to a curving gallery set with tableaux depicting a variety of horrific torments. Whispering voices gave graphic details while informing him that, for an extra fee, he could take advantage of the sensatapes which would allow him to experience the agonies of the victims.

A popular entertainment; each bench held customers, heads wreathed with silver bands, faces twisted as they suffered on a subjective plane. A place where Melome could have been but the tableaux were static models and Dumarest moved on.

To a hall where mirrors reflected his image in a thousand grotesque distortions.

To a misted cavern filled with invisible forces which caused him to sweat, to shiver, to feel the heat of passion and the chill disgust of self-contempt. To sigh and laugh and, with sudden fury, to scream curses.

A place yielding to another filled with drifting balloons which chuckled and cried, pleading, fuming, groaning, whimpering, tittering, sneering. Voices of suggestive intent and others mouthing abrasive insult. Hit, they burst to dispel sweet scents or acrid vapors. One clung, stinging, to his hand, the memory-plastic shriveling to mould itself into a plaque.

STUPID! The word it bore glowed with golden flame. It was followed by others, smaller; *"This token entitles you to a free gift."*

A blank-faced doll which he gave to a child gawking at a caged clown who mimicked the antics of a fierce and savage beast.

A gift easily disposed of but the accusation remained. Stupidly compounding his initial mistake—Melome would not be found by a frantic searching of public areas. She would need to be groomed, taught the finer arts of showmanship, tested to gauge her powers. Things he had overlooked in his urgent need to find her.

Dumarest slowed, turning at the sound of a bell. A girl with long raven hair, alabaster skin, a body shaped like an hourglass came slowly toward him. Her legs and arms were bare, a sequined dress hugging her figure with ebon brilliance. The bell was silver, its tone no sweeter than her voice.

"Get your tickets for the big show. Available at all barriers and booths. Half-price for children. Take your places for the most exciting, unusual, entertaining and overwhelming spectacle ever to be seen on Baatz. The performance will commence within the hour. Hurry! Hurry! Hurry!"

She halted as Dumarest touched her arm.

"I need help," he said, and swayed a little as he smiled; a man bemused a trifle but harmless enough. "I'm looking for a friend. She works for the circus but I can't seem to find her."

"Maybe she's off-duty, sir. Resting."

"I doubt it. She said to ask for her." He frowned, searching for a name. "Hilda. She said to ask for Hilda—no, Helga. That's it. Her name is Helga. Young, gold hair, nice smile. She was in town. On the boulevard. Advertising the circus. She said to be sure to ask for her and, well, here I am. You know her?"

She said, coldly, "Not personally. Ask an attendant to direct you to the information desk. They will send for her. If she's free she may meet you there."

She came after an hour, smiling, eyes searching his face. A mechanical smile and a look devoid of recognition; she must have spoken to more than a hundred men on the boulevard—he was just one of a crowd. Then, as she studied the neutral grey of his clothing, the lines and planes of his face, the smile changed, became warmer, more genuine.

"So it's you. I'm glad you came."

"That makes two of us. How long are you free?"

"For as long as you want—if you can pay."

22

"That's no problem." He smiled as he looked into her eyes, projecting his personality, his obvious admiration. "I've money and I'm in no hurry. But I am hungry and I guess you are too. Something to eat, maybe?"

"That would be nice."

"You'll make the food taste twice as good." He looked at her clothing, a simple dress belted at the waist, one devoid of ornamentation as was her throat, her wrists, her fingers. The bells and chains and displaying garment she had worn on the boulevard were for a different kind of work. "I've been lucky," he said. "And I like to share my good fortune. I'd also like you to remember me. Let's buy something to make sure you do that."

Smiling, she led him to a booth where he bought a bracelet of precious metal set with scintillant gems. An item worth the cost of a High passage but one he could afford. As he could afford the expensive meal, the wine, the liqueurs. Bribes augmented by his charm, his attention and courtesy so that later, in the privacy of her cubicle, she clung to him with genuine passion.

"Earl, my darling! Hold me! Hold me!"

She writhed in the circle of his arms, the warmth of her nudity burning against him, the softness of her flesh triggering his own desire so that it grew to dominate the universe, to flower, to fade in soft murmurings as her fingers searched his face, his naked body.

"A man, Earl. God, you're a man!"

"As you are a woman."

"Do you mean that? Do you really like me?"

"More than like you." He touched in turn and she sighed her pleasure, snuggling close to him. "You are a beautiful woman, Helga."

"Your woman, Earl."

"Mine."

She sighed again and walked her fingers over his torso, soft pads which traced the pattern of scars marring the skin. Old cicatrices; the medals of wounds won in the arena and visible proof of his skill and ability to survive.

"A fighter," she said. "Is that how you won your money?"

"Have you known many fighters?"

"A few."

"Here?"

"No," she was scornful. "Baatz is too soft. How did you get your money?"

He said, blandly, "How did you get to work for the circus?"

"Luck." She stretched against him, her hand sliding over his chest to the muscled plane of his stomach. "I developed fast and had a friend who told me to use what I had. The circus gave me an opportunity. I worked a dance routine for a while then settled for this." Her hand began to move in small circles. "And you?"

"I had a stake in a ship and sold out."

"A good deal?"

"The best." His arm closed around her. "Who buys for the circus?"

A question she ignored as her hand moved faster, lower, her chest heaving as her breath accelerated to a sudden, unaccustomed wave of desire.

"Earl!" Her lips found his own, pressed, fell moistly away. "You're wonderful. Such a man. A hero. So satisfying. Take me, darling. Take me!"

Mechanical words used in an automatic response but beneath them was something more. A feeling expressed by the movement of her body, the hunger of her lips even as she spoke the ritual of commercial love. Dumarest recognized it, knew that she was hampered by lack of true experience, unable to do more than use words and phrases learned by rote. A woman basically a stranger to love but learning and learning fast.

"Darling! Darling!" She heaved against him in demanding fury. "Hold me! Hold me, Earl! Hold me!"

Against the fears and terrors of the unknown; the frightening abyss which lay beyond the boundaries of mechanical sex. A region which demanded emotional surrender and gave in return a hint of paradise.

After, when again the fires had died and she lay snug in the crook of his arm, she said. "Did you mean it when you said you loved me?"

"Yes."

A moment then, as a statement, she said, "You've known a lot of women. You know too much not to have done. Did you love them?"

"Does it matter?"

"You loved them. You had to love them. Some men are like that; with them it's all or nothing. Others are like machines.

24

They aren't interested in you as a person but simply as a body to be used. There's a difference—God, what a difference!'' She reared to lean over him, breasts hanging like succulent fruit. ''Am I really your woman?''

For answer he stroked her hair.

''I'd be all you could ever want,'' she said. ''I promise that. And I wouldn't want anyone else but you, ever.''

A lie though she didn't know it; her own nature and intense femininity would drive her along the path she had chosen. To love and be loved—even the facsimile of true affection would govern her life.

Dumarest said, ''It's nice to think about, but don't you have commitments? A contract?''

''It can be broken. If you've enough money they'd let me go.''

The moment he'd been waiting for. He said, casually, ''It's a thought. Who would I have to see to make the deal?''

''I could arrange it.''

''No, things like that are best done personally.'' A smile made the remark innocuous, a smile he retained as he said, with equal casualness, ''How does it work? I mean, if someone's sold to the circus what happens to them?''

''They have to be trained. Washed, fed, dressed, healed sometimes and taught to walk and stand and smile.'' Her eyes narrowed a little. ''Why the interest?''

''Curiosity. I guess they must be kept in a special place. That dome with the false stairs?''

''That's the infirmary.'' She stooped to trail her breasts across his face. ''Kiss me, lover.''

He obliged. ''The one with the spirals?''

''You're close. Again.''

''Tell me.''

''It's next to the one you said.'' Straightening, she frowned. ''Why the interest?''

Dumarest shrugged. ''There could be money in it. A man I met in town has lost his daughter and thinks she may have been sold to the circus. He's willing to pay well to get her back.''

''His daughter?''

''That's what he said. She's young, bleached hair, thin, washed-out, half-starved. Her name's Melome. Maybe you've seen her.''

''No.''

"You could find out about her. Find out where she is. Fix it to buy her back."

Dumarest felt his anger rising as Helga shook her head. "Why not? Damn it, woman, why not?"

His anger betrayed him, was reflected in her face, her eyes, the rising tempo of her voice.

"You came here looking for her. Your girl. Lying to me. Using me. Making me feel I was something special. Promising—you bastard! You dirty bastard! Out! Get out! Out!"

"The girl!" Dumarest reared as she came at him, hands extended, fingers hooked, nails aiming at his eyes. "Melome! I—"

His hand thrust out in a defensive blow to save his eyes. The blow slammed against the woman's jaw and sent her rolling from the bed to lie shrieking on the floor.

"Rube! Rube! Hey Rube!"

The warning carny cry which spelled trouble and the need for help. Any circus worker within earshot would answer on the run.

Dumarest snatched at his clothes, found his knife, rose with it in his hand as men burst into the cubicle. Three of them armed with clubs. They halted as they saw the gleam of the blade, the man holding it in a fighter's stance. Their leader, a man with close-cropped hair and the massive bulk of a weight-lifter, glanced at the girl.

"Helga?"

"A pervert! The bastard hit me!"

"She's lying," said Dumarest. "If I hit her where's the mark?" The pad of his hand had cushioned the blow. "I'll leave but when I do I'll be dressed and walking." He turned the knife, light from the overhead lantern splintering from the steel, fuzzed on the edges and point. "Anyone have other ideas?"

"I'll handle this." The big man lowered his club as his companions left. To Dumarest he said, "I'll take you to a raft and, mister—don't ever try to come back!"

The shop was a cave of wonders; of ruffles and flounces, leather, plastic, feathers, belts glowing with filigree, garments heavy with fictitious gems. In the dim lighting the owner was a snuffling wasp who stared and shook his head in disapproval.

"A clown?"

"A clown." Dumarest was patient. "Nothing too elaborate. I

26

want to crash a party," he explained. "It's a fancy dress affair and I'm not too popular with the host. His wife, you understand." He saw the thin face crease in a frown and quickly adapted the story. "She doesn't like the plans I've made for her sister. If she hadn't interfered we'd have been married by now."

"An affair of the heart?" The costumer beamed, mollified. "But a clown?"

"It seems appropriate—all men in love are fools."

"True, but there is an art in these things. A soldier, now, or a great lord or a captain from space—you have the look and bearing of such. But a clown—who can take such seriously?"

"Exactly. You can supply me?"

"Of course. But you had better strip." The costumer gestured at the tuin Dumarest wore, high-collared, tight at the wrists, falling to mid-thigh. The pants and high boots. "The art of costume is to dress from the skin—only then can you really slip into the part."

"I'm not acting, just pretending, and I won't be wearing the costume for long. Could we hurry?"

Minutes later Dumarest left the shop, stooping, his head and face hidden by a grotesque mask, his clothing by a loose garment of ragged tatters. One which led to flared pants trailing the ground and all in blotches of vibrant color. He swayed as he moved toward the area where the circus rafts were kept, using a bottle to daub himself with alcohol.

It was past midnight and the area was apparently deserted, but as he reached it a shape loomed from the shadows.

"You there! What do you want?"

"A ride." Dumarest halted, swaying, lurching closer to the guard. "Gotta get back to the cus . . . cir . . . gotta get back."

"You're drunk." The guard wrinkled his nose at the reek of spirit. "Stinking. Why don't you sleep it off?"

"Gotta get back."

"Sure. Tomorrow at first light." The clown was of the circus and the circus looked after its own. "Bed down in a raft." He gestured toward the grounded vehicles and laughed. "Pick a soft one."

Dumarest picked the one farthest from the light falling over the rail, muttering, changing the mutter to a snore. He heard the crunch of boots as the guard came to check and sensed the impact of the man's eyes. Satisfied he turned away and Dumarest relaxed, unclenching his hand, opening his eyes to look at the stars. They were blotched by patches of cloud but clear enough to check their wheeling. A clock which measured time for the guard to relax and fall into a doze. For the circus to bed down for the night.

The raft was locked, the key missing, as Dumarest had expected. The knife whispered from his boot and eased away the casing over the control panel. Wires lay exposed, black in the starlight, and he traced them with his fingers to select two pairs. Insulation shredded beneath the edge of the blade. A twist and the vehicle became alive.

Dumarest sent it upwards, rising like a shadow, soundless save for the hum from the antigrav units. A good vehicle and well-maintained—the circus could not afford accidents. When the town had fallen far below and the boulevard was a thin streak of brilliance he sent it toward the place where Melome would be waiting.

A short journey but one longer by night and he strained his eyes, searching the hills, grunting his relief as, far to the left, he saw the glow of massed bubbles. Poor navigation and he corrected it, swinging wide so as to approach from the far side. The lights were dim, the glow a pearly sheen which hid sharp detail, and he halted the raft as he examined his target.

Where had Helga said?

He thinned his lips as he remembered the woman, the incident her jealousy had caused. His own fault—he should have remembered the double standard of those who followed her profession. The sudden tempers and demanding passion. The brittle emotions and fierce possessiveness, but his own urgency had made him careless.

Where had she said?

A dome moved before him as he touched the controls; one daubed with lozenges of color now dulled by starlight. A walk which wasn't real, a sweeping arch, a winding path, a spire—all the products of illusion. A minaret circled with a staircase. . . .

Stairs?

The infirmary, Helga had said—would Melome be there? The woman hadn't said and, at the time, she'd no reason to lie. There, perhaps? There?

Again the raft moved and Dumarest narrowed his eyes. Starlight and shadows altered perspective and robbed colors of distinctive hues. Was that dome white with red spirals or black with white? Close, Helga had said; the place he wanted was close to a spiraled dome. But which?

He had to take a chance. To drift was to invite discovery. The raft dropped as he made his decision, softly, lightly, coming to rest on taut membrane, indenting it, the plastic rising as he adjusted the lifting units. A delicate balance but shielding domes would protect it from any wind and those same domes would keep it hidden from the ground.

Dumarest left the raft and looked around. He'd landed on the roof of what he assumed to be a gallery; part of a convex web lying between soaring domes. One close to him was ridged in a pattern of fluted columns, another, smaller, bore snarling beast-masks, the mouths ugly with fangs. He left them behind as he walked to where the web branched, halting as he reached the target he had chosen; a cone which held a steady rustling, one set with a ladder that was real.

A vent, he guessed, or an induction tube feeding the pumps which maintained the internal pressure. The gilded summit would hold filters and the ladder was to allow access. The place should have a door yielding to inner mechanisms, and he found it on the far side, a narrow panel which jerked open to reveal a dimly lit interior filled with a louder murmuring and the scent of dust.

From below came the sound of voices.

". . . had about enough. If Zucco pushes me much harder I'll quit."

"That's your privilege, but he's not so bad."

"He's an animal. Well, to hell with him. Playing tonight?"

"I'm bushed and the luck's against me. I'm for the sack."

Odd scrapings rose above the murmuring; tools being set in their place, Dumarest guessed, or cans being moved. The men could be roustabouts on cleaning or maintenance duty, tired now, careless, but it would be a mistake to take that for granted. Yet to find another entry would take too much time. The external membrane was too tough to slit and, even if he slashed an opening, air loss would register.

Dumarest stripped off the clown's mask and costume; if the circus had bedded down it would arouse attention and would hamper quick movement. Stairs led down from where he stood and he moved down them, freezing as something moved at their foot. His face was in shadow, the grey of his clothing blending with the wall behind him—only movement would betray him.

He saw the blur of a face looking upwards, the hand which reached for the rail.

"Leave it, Brad." The other man, invisible, echoed his fatigue. "We'll sweep out tomorrow. Come on—I've had enough."

The face vanished, the hand, and Dumarest heard the pad of boots, a sighing rustle, then silence. Cautiously he moved to the floor below. The air-vent passed through it and from the vibration he guessed the pumps were below. Brooms, cans, dusters stood racked against a wall together with loose coveralls and peaked caps. He donned one, slipped a loose coat over his shoulders and picking up a broom, pushed his way through the rollers of an air-trap.

Beyond lay the curve of a gallery, another door, a room holding tables, chairs, people.

Circus folk at recreation.

Men for the most part though women were among them, all casually dressed, none in costume though some bore the traces of makeup. Cards, bottles, plates of small cakes stood on the tables and, on the far side, a man swore as he rolled dice.

"Six again—damn the luck! Three times down in a row!"

A woman said, "Give it up, Sakai. Lose more and you'll be paying to work."

"That'll be the day—there's always the punters."

"Try lifting their cash and you'll be out on your butt." The woman, a hard-eyed, hard-faced brunette with skin raddled beneath her paint, poured more wine into her glass. To Dumarest she said, "Hey! Come to sweep us out?"

He grimaced, lifting the broom, pointing ahead.

"Swamping, eh? Rather you than me. Say, you new here?"

He nodded, gesturing with the broom again, acting the mute. To talk would lead to conversation which could betray him.

A man called, "Guide him right, Zulme."

"Sure." She pointed to a door to the left. "Through there, swamper. Then the first door to your right. Clean good, now, or Draba will be after your tail."

Laughter followed Dumarest as he left the room. A short passage lay before him and he passed the door to his right. Then one led to something he chose to avoid—the laughter had lacked true humor and he guessed the woman had made him the butt of a joke. An air-trap ended the passage and he squeezed through it, scenting the sudden acridity of the air. An odor which strengthened as he reached a door, cracked it open, passed through into a soft dimness.

"Melome?" She could be asleep, resting—the place was where he judged she might be. "Melome?"

Then, suddenly, he was fighting for his life.

CHAPTER THREE

———⚫◆⚫———

It came from the shadows, a blow which tore the peaked cap from his head, raking downwards to shred the loose coat from his shoulders. One which would have torn the scalp from his head had Dumarest not acted with unthinking speed. A stir of the air warned him, a gust of fetid odor, the sense of movement and he was moving forward and down to cushion the blow which slammed against his back. Feeling the impact of it. The grate, as claws ripped into his tunic to meet the protective mesh buried in the plastic.

The metal saved him from crippling lacerations but he felt the bruising fury, the shock, the force driving him to the floor.

He rolled as he hit, rolled again as something struck close enough to sting his eyes with wind. Something looming monstrous in the gloom, a shape of hair and limbs and a squatly huge body. One with claws and fangs gleaming with a greenish phosphorescence.

A beast spawned on some radiation-lashed world now snarling with a killing rage.

It lunged forward, foot raised to kick, taloned nails to rip out Dumarest's stomach and spill his intestines. A blow which would kill even if the mesh held, rupturing the spleen, pulping liver. A blow which missed as he flung himself over the floor, rising to back, almost falling as his foot hit the broom.

A weapon he snatched up and poised, bristles forward, the points aimed at the back-sloping face, the eyes. A thrust and he dodged the reaching claws, darting to one side as the thing pawed at its sockets. A minor irritation and it snarled as again Dumarest attacked, snatching at the broom, snapping off the head to leave him with a splintered stick.

A broken spear less than five feet long.

One he lashed upwards, feeling the tug of a claw in his hair as he hit the crotch, the genitals resting between the massive thighs. Ducking to stab at the same target. Backing as saliva and stench gushed from the fanged mouth.

After a moment of respite Dumarest checked the area. The door by which he had entered the room was barred by the thing facing him but another lay to one side. The room itself was illuminated by a single glowing plate set in the ceiling. A mass of straw lay in one corner, a trough in another. One containing water, he guessed, a bowl, now empty, could have held food.

A snarl and the creature lunged toward him. Clearly it had learned; the long arms hung protectively over the crotch, one lifting as it came close, the clawed paw missing as Dumarest darted aside. A move which gave him a choice of either door, but the one by which he had entered led only back the way he had come.

He spun, dropping to one knee, the wooden shaft in his hands whining as he sent it in a savage blow to the creature's leg. A blow which hit the kneecap, shattering the wood, but hampering the beast long enough for Dumarest to reach the other door. To duck through it. To slam it fast.

He leaned his back against it as he fought for breath.

Before him stretched a chamber, narrow, set with a guard rail before flanking cubicles with raised floors. Rooms like cells but without the bars. In the nearest something stirred.

At first he thought it a large bird then it turned and Dumarest saw the undoubted humanity behind the elongated jaws which gave the impression of a beak, the rounded, avian eyes, the double-orifice where a nose should have been. An illusion heightened by the extended column of the neck, the lack of ears, the backward slope of the forehead. Vivid tattooing supplied an artificial plumage.

As he stepped forward the creature retreated, hopping on distorted feet, thin, curved fingers lifting in futile protection. A quasi-human, naked, slight, unmistakably female.

"Don't touch her!" The voice was a deep gurgle coming from a cubicle opposite. "Leave her alone. You frighten her, Gora, and I'll—" The voice paused. "Gora?"

"No." Dumarest turned to face a bloated obscenity; a man so gross as to be repulsive. Like the bird-girl he was naked. "Who is Gora?"

"Someone I'll kill one day. If he gets within reach of my hands. If I can get my teeth in his throat. Come closer—I can't see so good. Who are you? Your aura's strange."

"It's mine. Who are you?"

"Rastic Alatabani Seglar. Call me Ras. Would you believe I was handsome once?" The massive bulk shook with either laughter or tears. "A traveler. A kid with stars in his eyes. I had the universe to rove in but I chose the wrong world. Got contaminated. Began to swell. Money would have saved me but I had no cash. Now I can't move. If I wasn't with the circus I'd die."

A product of disease, disfigured, almost blind. Dumarest looked at the caricature of a face, the filmed orbs. A freak as the bird-girl was a freak, and the man tufted with feathers in the next cubicle, and the woman lower down—the one with two heads.

"I'm Olga," said one. "My, you're handsome. Tall and strong and a real man. More than Ras ever was, I'll bet. He lies, you know. Lies all the time."

"Like you," said the other head. "I'm Inez. Pay no attention to her. She's jealous. She thinks everyone who comes to see us is interested only in her. Tell the truth, now, aren't I the prettiest?"

Dumarest said, "Maybe you can help me. I'm looking for a friend."

"A girl! I bet it's a girl!"

"Shut up, Olga! You talk too much!"

"And you eat too much! You're making me fat! Soon I'll be as ugly as you are!"

"Bitch!"

"Cow!"

"Shut up!" A harsh voice roared from the end of the chamber. "Cut that babbling or I'll do it for you! You hear me? Cut it out!"

"Gora!" Olga sucked in her breath. "Inez—do as he says."

"I'm not afraid of him."

"I am. Now be quiet."

Their voices faded to twitterings as Dumarest walked to the far end of the chamber. Past a cubicle from which something stared at him, faceless, sexless beneath the thick mat of hair covering it from scalp to toes. Feeling the eyes of a woman with multiple breasts, another with a hump topped by a squinting, elfin face. A man with scales and vestigial wings. One thick with warty encrustations. A score of distorted human shapes.

Gora looked like a dog.

He sat in the far cubicle, lips sagging, jowls, the pouches of his eyes. Pointed ears added to the resemblance and his hair, fine and russet, covered forehead, neck, face and body. Pointed teeth gleamed as he bared his lips.

"Artificial," he said. "But the customers like it."

"You in charge here?"

"I try to keep some sort of order. I've the voice for it." He deepened his tone to a snarling growl, one terminating in a bark. "That's acting—the rest is real. Genetic disorder, myasthenia, myopathy—you a doctor?"

"No."

"Then you wouldn't be interested. A freak-nut, then? Come to indulge yourself? Wanting to see how we behave when not performing?" The liquid eyes studied Dumarest. "No, I guess not. What, then? Grag wouldn't have passed you unless you were straight." He looked at the door through which Dumarest had come. "Conditioned to stay in his room," he explained. "But without the whistle he'll kill without warning."

"A watchdog?"

"Something like that. Keeps us in and others out. Too rough for showing but he has his uses. Which is more than you can say for the rest of us."

"Including you?"

"I do what I can. I'd go crazy if I didn't. At times I think I'm crazy anyway and it gets worse when we're not on show. Then, sometimes, it's possible to think of the marks as freaks and us as normal. Their eyes, the way they goggle, grin, act. Talking as if we were deaf, acting as if we couldn't see, poking with sticks, making suggestions, speculating how we come to be as we are." The artificial fangs gleamed as Gora snarled. "Throwing us bones, candy, filth. They must be sick in the head."

Dumarest said, "Is this all there are of you?"

"Freaks? Why be afraid of the word? That's what we are— freaks. Some born that way, some growing, others made. You think I'm joking?"

"No," said Dumarest.

"That spider-man over there. Can you guess how his arms and legs got that long? Babies are malleable. Tissue can be stretched, bone too when you're young and mostly gristle. They rested him on a plank and tied weights to his wrists and ankles. Heavy weights left for years. Something to see when he was ready." Gora spat his disgust. "People!"

Dumarest made no comment.

"So we sit here," continued Gora. "Amusing the normal. Taking their insults, sometimes their pity. At times I don't know which is worse."

"I do," said Dumarest. "One freak bullying another, for example."

"I don't bully them."

"Ras wants to kill you."

"Ras wants to die," corrected the dog-man. "At times we all want to die. How else can we escape this hell?"

"You're fed, housed, kept warm," reminded Dumarest. "So you have to earn it—but who else would employ you? Some would think you are lucky. And if you want to die you can do it whenever you want."

"How? Without a gun? A knife?" Gora looked at the hilt riding above Dumarest's boot. "You could do it. Give me an easy way out."

"No, I won't do that. Any edge will do. Teeth if you've nothing else. Just bite through a vein."

"That all?"

"That's all—if you've the guts." Dumarest watched as Gora lifted his wrist to his mouth, the fangs lowering, biting, indentations showing on the hair, the flesh beneath. Before blood could flow he said, quickly, "You've the courage but you're not ready yet. When you are you'll do it fast. But you know the others need you."

An out the other accepted. "Yes," he said, lowering his wrist. "Yes, I guess they do."

"You help them all the time."

"That's right."

"And you can help me. I'm looking for a girl named Melome. She was sold to the circus last night."

"A freak?"

"A sensitive." Dumarest added, "Some would call it the same thing."

"They could be right." Gora shook his head. "I haven't seen her. Try the infirmary." He gestured at the door close to his cubicle. "You'll have to go out that way." As Dumarest reached for the knob he said, "Would it hurt?"

"Just the sting of the bite. After that you'd just drift into sleep."

Into sleep and death and final oblivion. An easy way out—but one Dumarest would never take.

Reiza snapped, "Up, Chang! Up!"

He was slow to respond, snuffing the air, lambent eyes shifting in the sleek perfection of his skull. Small signs others might have overlooked or ignored but to her they were beacons of danger. Attention diffused when it should have been concentrated solely on her. The crack of her whip demanded attention.

"Stay!" The animal had moved a little. "Stay, Chang! Stay!"

A beast troubled by unaccustomed stimuli; during the last performance some fool had chosen to use a klaxon. A trick which had raised a laugh but which had almost shattered the delicate balance of command she held over her charges. An unthinking gesture, perhaps, or maybe one with a sinister intent; placid though Baatza was yet there were always those yearning for violence and the sight of blood.

"Up!" The crack of her whip again. "Up, Chang! Up!"

Again the obedience was slow though others wouldn't have noticed the delay. The mating season? Had the stir of hormones made the beast restless? A possibility and one she would check using drugs to gain tranquility if they were needed. A procedure she would rather avoid; drugged animals lacked the sharp edge which enhanced the performance.

"Reiza?" Zucco spoke from the shadows, the seats behind him rising in a tiered array to circle the ring. "Will you be much longer?"

A question which irritated her; rehearsals and training took as long as was necessary.

"You're tired," he said, stepping forward. "It's been a long day and—"

"Stay clear!" The crack of her whip emphasized the command. "Damn it, Jac, you know better than to interfere at a time like this. Chang's edgy enough as it is. That fool with the klaxon—"

"I threw him out."

"But the damage was done. Now leave me." She saw the movement of the beast's eyes, the tensing of muscle beneath the ebon fur. "Leave me!"

He obeyed and yet still something was wrong. Not just her fatigue or the drifting attention of the animal but something else.

A conflict of wills on a primordial level, one Hayter had warned her about before he had died, his face ripped from the bone beneath, intestines spilling from opened bowels.

"Never take them for granted, Reiza. Cats look calm and placid but always they are a danger. A whim and you could be dead. The blow might be struck in anger or for sport—but you are still dead."

Just as he was dead, as were others she had known, but she would not be one of them.

"Chang!" An animal to be dominated and she felt the surge of anger rising within her. A radiated determination which eliminated the possibility of disobedience. "Down! Down!"

The crack of the whip, showmanship when giving a performance but in reality signals the creature obeyed. The punctuation of her verbal commands, repeated as, dutifully, the animal dropped from the stool, mounted another, stepped through a hoop, squatted like some ancient deity.

And, again, snuffed at the air.

"You!" Reiza turned, saw a glimpse of white, the hint of movement. "You there!"

"Me?" Dumarest halted, shifting the bundle beneath his arm; a mass of paper and rag he'd wrapped close to form a package. One which a casual glance would assume he was delivering. "You want me?"

"Come closer!"

She stood waiting as he approached, straddle-legged, the whip dangling from her right wrist. Tall, strong, a mane of black hair cut to reach her shoulders. A color matched by the halter she wore, the shorts, the boots which rose to mid-thigh, accentuating the creamy whiteness of her skin. Above the naked midriff her breasts bulged against the thin plastic of their prison.

She said, "You're new here, right?"

"Yes, but—"

"You smell wrong. Chang noticed it. Weren't you warned about coming into the main ring?" Her eyes searched his face, his clothing, her own nostrils flaring. "You stink."

The saliva sprayed by the ape-thing guarding the freaks. A scent caught now by the woman as it had disturbed the beast. As Dumarest watched it moved, sickle-claws gleaming from velvet pads, fangs showing between lifted lips.

A black leopard; rearing, it would be as tall as a man. A killing machine holding the beauty of functional design.

He said, "I shouldn't leave that animal alone too long."

"You're teaching me my business?"

"Giving you some advice. You—"

"Keep it." She was scornful. "Who the hell are you, anyway? A swamper? What are you doing here?"

Questions he'd so far managed to avoid. A man with a package, moving with purposeful determination—those he'd met had assumed he belonged. But the infirmary had been empty and Melome had still to be found.

"It's my sister," he said. "I'm bringing her a few things."

"Your sister?"

"That's right. She joined the circus last night and forgot to take a few essentials." He gestured with the package. "Maybe you know her? A sensitive. If I could just have a word with her?"

"You're lying!" Reiza was curt. "If you don't belong you've no right to be wandering around. What's in that package? Stuff you've stolen? Is that what you are; a lousy thief? And that smell—what the hell have you been up to?"

"Nothing." Dumarest backed away. "Nothing at all. I'll just get away, now. Leave you to it."

He turned and took three steps toward the shadows when he heard the woman's sharp command.

"Chang! Hold!"

One which sent the leopard hurtling from where it squatted.

Dumarest turned, jumping to one side, the package lifting, lancing toward the snarling mask. A distraction the leopard ignored, landing, springing again as Dumarest reached for his knife, feeling his foot slip on something in the sand, toppling, feeling the slamming impact of the animal as he went down. Pinned, helpless, he stared into the snarling mask.

And froze.

Reiza said, "At least you've the sense not to move. A hunter?" As Dumarest made no reply she added, "You're playing dead. Hoping Chang will get bored and move away. In the wild that might work if you aren't bleeding and the beast isn't starving." She leaned over him, nostrils flared, sniffing. "You stink but not of fear. That's good. All right, Chang, back now." Her tone hardened. "Back, Chang! Back!"

Dumarest sat upright as the beast left, seeing it lope toward the shadows, its caged den. He climbed to his feet as the woman turned to face him.

"A thief," she said. "Certainly a liar." The lash of her whip tore at the package. "A few things for your sister? It holds nothing but rubbish." The lash cracked an inch from his cheek. "Talk, damn you!"

"I came looking for someone. A girl. Melome. That's all."

"Your sweetheart?" The whip cracked again and he felt a sting on his cheek. Touching it, he saw blood on his fingers. "You like her?"

As she liked what she was doing, the whip, the questions, the usage of power. Dominating him. Playing with him as a cat would torment a mouse. And there was more than a little of the feline about her. In the slant of her eyes, the set of her mouth. The whip was a claw she sent to sting.

"Thief! Liar! Why are you here?"

"I told you. I'm—" Dumarest looked at the welt she put on the back of his hand. It burned like fire. "Be careful with that whip."

"I could take out your eyes. Have one lying on your cheek before you knew it." Already she had proved it to be no idle boast. "Cut off your ears. Flay you. Slice open your face. Do you think I wouldn't?"

"I think you'd enjoy doing it."

"So?"

"Don't touch me with that whip again!"

A warning rejected. Dumarest saw the widening of her eyes, the movement of her hand and was moving before the lash could strike. A spring toward her, his right hand snatching at his boot to rise weighted with nine inches of pointed, razor edged steel. His left arm shot out, the hand gripping the lash as the blade sliced upwards to sever it inches from the stock.

"You!" Startled, she looked at the knife, the ruined whip. "Bastard!" Anger replaced the amazement. The stock parted in her hand, became a falling sheath and a foot-long stiletto which she held like a sword in her hand. Its point lanced toward his eyes.

Dumarest parried it with a clash of metal, attacked in turn, air whining as his blade slashed in a vicious arc. One aimed at the throat, the jugular it contained, the life-blood it carried. A blow dictated by reactive instinct. One changed almost too late to send the point of the knife slashing downwards. Leather parted as it sliced through the halter to free her breasts and leave a shallow gash on the creamy skin.

Then she was his prisoner, his left arm rising beneath her right, his fingers locked in the mane of her hair. Pulling back her head and exposing her throat to the prick of his blade.

"You—"

"Shut up!" The point dug deeper, almost breaking the skin. "You had your fun and now it's my turn. I could blind you," he said, mimicking her threats. "Slash your face. Cut off your nose. Do you think I wouldn't?"

She swallowed. "What do you want?"

"Melome. Take me to her."

"The girl? I don't know where she is."

"Then find out." Impatience edged his voice with the raw note of anger. "Someone bought her. Someone must know where she is. Now move. Move!"

He shifted to stand behind her, his hand still locked in her hair, the knife still at her throat. A position maintained as he urged her over the sand of the ring toward the tiered seats.

The passage, the men who were waiting, the gas which sent him spinning into oblivion.

Zucco had given her a lamp; a thing of delicate artistry depicting a woman locked in a feline's embrace, the whole illuminated from within. By its light Reiza examined herself in a mirror.

She was nude, skin still damp from a scented bath, the thick mane of her hair framing her face and edging her shoulders. A good body, one still firm, muscles clothed by softening fat which enhanced her unabashed femininity. One untouched by claw or fang—luck and skill had seen to that; the costume she wore was for show and not concealment. But now she had been marked and her hand lifted to touch the gash on her breastbone. One about an inch long, shallow; healed it would leave no trace. But, always, within her mind she would bear the scar.

The scar and the man who had injured her.

Closing her eyes she could see him again. The face hard, cold, the mask of an animal. A creature determined to survive. One ready to kill to avoid being killed. Like Chang and Ahrda and Torin. Like all the great cats she had trained—his eyes had matched theirs. His reflexes had been as fast. Faster—never had she known a man move so quickly. Death had been very close.

And, again, she felt the thrill of it.

A moment Hayter had mentioned when, satiated, he had lain beside her in a place redolent of the cats they both loved.

"It's the power," he'd said. "The dominance. To rule over creatures which could kill you without hesitation if the mood took them. But over that is the thrill of danger. Each time you train or perform you risk your life. Take a gamble—your skill against their instincts. It's like a drug which, for a moment, makes you more than human. Makes you come really alive. And, always, there is the temptation to push your luck a little harder. To tempt fate a little more. Don't do it, Reiza. When it comes to that, quit the game."

Advice he hadn't taken—had he welcomed the claws which had ripped out his life? The attack which had saved him from descrepit old age?

She hoped it had been like that. He had been too full of life to waste and fade. Too proud to be other than the best in his field. And, when her time came, would she feel the same as when death had come so close?

The knife slashing at her throat—time had seemed to slow to extend the moment and, against her lids, she could see the glitter of steel, the edge and point. Feel again the constriction of her stomach, the anticipation. Then the burn, her breasts falling free, the sting of the knife at her throat.

And the face so close to her own.

A chime and she ŏpened her eyes, swaying a little. The effects of the gas had been neutralized but traces lingered and she caught the edge of the mirror to steady herself.

"Reiza?" Zucco's voice and, again, the chime. As always he was impatient. "Reiza? Are you all right?"

"A moment." A robe lay close and she donned it, yellow silk, rich in the diffused illumination. Material which held a sensuous appeal and it clung to her body as she tied it around her waist. "Enter!"

He walked like a cat, light on the balls of his feet, his body slender, lithe, bright with scarlet and gold. Garments modeled on those worn in the ring lacking only the cheap glitter of sequins and artificial gems. His face, thinned, held the sharp awareness of a predator. His eyes held the darting flicker of a serpent's tongue.

"My dear!" He halted before her, tall, showing an outward concern. "Are you sure you're all right? The gas—"

"Did you have to use it?"

43

"There was no other way. Shot he could have killed you as he fell. Threatened—" His shrug was expressive. "Your life was too valuable to risk."

And so the gas kept by for use in emergencies against animals running wild, men, crowds.

"A madman," he said. "Deranged. He could have killed you."

Would have done had he really wanted. Zucco, watching from the shadows, had not seen the initial lethal aim of the blade, the sudden withdrawal.

She said, "Did you find out who he is?"

"Dumarest. Earl Dumarest. He was at the circus earlier and Ruval had to throw him out. Some trouble over a girl. One of Tusenbach's. It could have been settled but he drew a knife and left Ruval no choice."

"Melome?" She saw his frown. "He spoke of a sister he'd come to see. Melome. Was that the girl?"

"He lied."

"About the girl?"

"She isn't his sister. He asked after her before and then she was the daughter of a friend. Forget her." He stepped closer, hands reaching, his intention plain. As she stepped back he said, impatiently, "What's wrong?"

"Nothing."

"Then why avoid me? Or do you want to play a game?" His eyes glowed with a new fire, his face taking on a feral expression, a gloating anticipation. "You want to be mastered, forced, made to yield to the whip? Dominated? Treated like you treat your cats? Given a taste of pain."

Things he enjoyed but her needs were not governed by a sadistic nature. One he possessed, now rising to be mirrored on his face as he stared at her, stimulated by her femininity, her reluctance.

She said, quickly, "What about the girl? Melome. Is she with the circus?"

"I told you to forget her."

"Something special?"

"That isn't your business. Just worry about your cats and leave the rest to me. Ask questions and Shakira won't like it. Now let's stop wasting time." He frowned as she shook her head. "No? Why not?"

"Be sensible, man. I'm tired. I've been gassed and am still

groggy. And I've had a hell of an experience. All I want now is to be left alone to sleep.''

A lie and he sensed it as he sensed her heightened sensuality: emotions inflamed and sharpened by recent events. As he moved purposefully toward her she stepped to one side, reaching her spare costume, the flat pistol normally worn in a holster beneath the shorts. A gun she hadn't bothered to carry when dealing with a single animal. One she lifted to point at Zucco's face.

''I said no, Jac.''

He halted, staring at the twin muzzles of the over and under; wide orifices which could spout a leaden hail.

''You'd use that? Against me?'' Her eyes gave him the answer. ''Bitch! I thought we were friends.''

''We are,'' she agreed. ''That and more. But you don't own me. I don't dance to your tune. We'll get on better if you remember that.'' Lowering the gun she added, casually, ''What happened to Dumarest?''

''He's safe enough.''

''Dead?''

''Would you care if he was?'' His eyes searched her face, his own hardening as they moved to the gap in her robe, the wound lying between her breasts. ''He cut you, remember. Marked you.''

Branded her—there was a difference.

She said, ''I'm curious. He acted strange. He's safe, you say?''

''Safe.'' Zucco's smile held malice. ''He's down in the sump.''

CHAPTER FOUR

Dumarest woke to the stench of it, the dirt, the noise. The circus was a closed world of inflated tents, domes, galleries, compartments. One holding animals, workers, a continual flow of visitors. A close-packed consuming society—the sump took care of the waste.

A place of dimness in which sewage and garbage was dumped to be fed to machines which churned it and fed the slurry to pipes leading outside. There was leakage, accumulations, pools of slime. Maintenance workers wore enclosing suits and breathed tanked air.

Dumarest, naked, was chained to a wall.

His head ached from the effects of the gas and thirst burned throat and mouth. In the gloom things looked blurred, out of focus, and he closed his eyes, palming them, feeling the tug and clank of restraining links. Manacles circled each wrist, the chains from them running through a circlet on the metal belt locked around his waist. Another chain at the rear led to a ring on the wall.

He could stand, take a step forward, lie on the crusted floor and that was all.

A prisoner sentenced without trial to a period of isolated confinement. One which could be the prelude to execution. It was possible, the circus was a law unto itself. A hostile world in which he was a stranger. For now he could do nothing but wait.

Squatting, he examined the links. They were too strong to break, welded, made of high-grade steel. The manacles were too close fitting to slip and prevented him reaching the chain holding him to the wall. A futile exercise; it too would be strong.

Something ran over his foot and he saw a blur of chiton as a multilegged insect scuttled toward a patch of crusted slime. Food and water for the thing but only vileness for himself. Yet the creature was food and could be eaten if starvation threatened. But, before that, he would be dead of thirst.

The wall behind him was of metal and he touched it, feeling the dew of condensation. Moisture he collected on the flat of his hand, licking it, wiping the metal to gain more. It held a flat, unpleasant taste but it moistened his lips and eased his thirst a little. Relaxing he leaned his back against the wall.

Waiting, dozing, conserving his strength. Jerking to full awareness as metal clanged and a light shone into his eyes.

"So you're awake." Zucco, his finery protected by a plastic film, lifted the wand he carried. One tipped with metal. Dumarest jerked at the sting of it against his flesh. "Hurts, doesn't it." The voice held a feral purr as it came through the diaphragm of the helmet. "A thing we use on beasts to teach them to obey." It stabbed again. "Like this. And this. And this."

A series of nerve-jarring shocks as the current tore at his body. Through a red haze of pain Dumarest twisted, fought the restraint of the chains, the instinct which urged him to snatch at the wand. Even if he gained it he would have won nothing. Not until the man himself was within reach dare he act.

"Why did you come here?" The wand hit again before Dumarest could answer, touching his knee, his stomach, dropping to his loins. "Answer, you scum. Answer!"

Crude interrogation; questions followed by pain and then more questions with no time given for answers. A technique designed to break the spirit and induce unthinking responses.

Cowering, Dumarest said, "Melome! I came for the girl!"

The cowering was an act, the answer genuine; one he had given before.

"Why?" Again the wand. "Why? Why? Why?"

"A job." Dumarest gagged, pointing at his mouth. "Water! Give me water!"

"After you talk." The wand seared nerves and filled the universe with pain. "The truth, now! Damn it, I want the truth!"

"You've had it. I wanted a job. I figured Melome could give me an introduction to the boss. Someone who could hire me."

"So you came here, sneaked into the circus, crept about like a thief, attacked Reiza and would have killed her—just to get hired?'' Zucco sneered his contempt. "Do you take me for a fool?''

"No—a sadistic bastard!"

Zucco tensed with anger, face taut, as he raised the wand, holding it like a rapier, the metal tip circling inches from Dumarest's eyes.

"Now we're getting somewhere," he whispered. "I knew you couldn't be broken so easily. But you will be broken. Made to beg. To crawl." The wand jabbed forward, touched, touched again. Bruising impacts which lacked the previous searing energy; Zucco had deactivated the instrument. "Odd," he said. "Reiza said you were fast. Fast enough to have dodged but—" This time Dumarest jerked as Zucco fed power to the wand, sent the tip to jab a shoulder. "Talk!"

"Water!"

"Talk, damn you! Talk! Talk! Talk!"

A man beside himself with rage, converting it to pleasure, enjoying the pain he caused, the anguish. One who would kill unless satisfied; his need justification enough for any action he chose to take.

Dumarest jerked, slumped to the floor, feeling the bite of nails in his palms as he clenched his fists. Screaming to vent his rage at the pain which consumed him, a sound Zucco mistook for terror, the signal of his victory.

Panting he stepped back, lowering the wand, looking at the slumped figure before him. A man sprawled in a faint and beyond any further pain he could inflict.

"I'll be back," he said. "And, when I do, you won't escape so easily. Ruval!"

Dumarest heard the pad of boots as Zucco moved away. More footsteps came close, heavier, accompanied by a metallic clinking. He gasped as a flood of water drenched head and shoulders. Another and he rose upright to stare at a massive body, a close-cropped head. One he had seen before.

"Here!" Ruval handed him a beaker of water. "I warned you not to come back but you had to be smart. Crazy to do what you did. Now you're paying for it."

Dumarest handed back the empty container. "Your doing?"

"Zucco's. The one who questioned you. Reiza's his woman. You made a mistake going up against her."

"And you?"

"I just work here." Ruval refilled the beaker and handed it to Dumarest. "Gas makes you thirsty and you've enough trouble as it is."

"Thanks." Dumarest sipped, looking at the big man. Less kind than he seemed; Zucco must have given him orders to take care of his charge. To get him in condition for another session with the wand. "Is Zucco the boss?"

"The ringmaster."

"But not the owner?" As Ruval shook his head Dumarest added, "You said something about paying. I can pay. A thousand kobolds if you help me get out of here."

"Forget it."

"Why? All you need is the key. A file if you can't get it. I've money on deposit in town. It's yours if you'll help. A thousand in cash." Money which would buy luxury. Dumarest watched as the man's interest grew. "What can you lose?" he urged. "Think of what you could buy."

Ruval said, "How would you pay?"

"I'll give you a note. The money will be put aside. You can see it, check that it's there. When I sign the transfer it'll be yours."

"Sign?"

"Countersign. Of course, I'll have to be with you at the time. A thousand kobolds." Dumarest emphasized the figure. "How long would it take you to earn that much?"

Too long, but there were problems.

"I don't know," said Ruval. "I'm just not sure."

"Afraid of Zucco? You could break him in half with one hand. Doubt my word? Talk to Helga, she'll tell you I've money. I didn't hurt her, you know. I wasn't lying."

"I didn't figure you were. A push, a slap, touch them in the wrong way, even, and they scream murder." Ruval sucked at his cheeks. "A thousand?"

"That's right."

"Just for bringing you a file?"

"For getting me out of here," corrected Dumarest. "I want to be free and clear."

He sipped at the water as the man thought about it. Ruval was dressed in good clothing; pants of good weave and boots of fine leather. His blouse was ornamented by a cluster of brilliant stones held to the fabric by a long pin. His belt was carved in elaborate designs. A chain around his neck held a massive lucky charm. A dandy despite his bulk. One who would always need money.

"Well?"

Ruval shook his head. "I daren't risk it. Zucco would have my hide."

"Two thousand then. Double."

"No."

"Coward!" Dumarest blazed with anger. "You stinking freak! You've no guts!"

He flung the beaker into Ruval's face.

It hit above an eye, shattering, breaking the skin to mask the face with blood. Ruval snarled and lunged forward, fists clenched, slamming like hammers at Dumarest's face and body. Blows he tried to divert, dissipating their force as he grappled with the big man, but enough landed to make him grunt with shock and pain. To fall and lie slumped in a limp heap.

"Scum!" Ruval drove his boot into the naked body. "I treat you decent and what do I get? To hell with you!"

He stormed away leaving Dumarest lying bleeding, semi-conscious, the gemmed pin he had stolen clutched tightly in his hand.

It was going all wrong.

Reiza, standing in the brilliant circle of light, alone with her animals, sensed it with the instinct which made her what she was. Chang was too slow to obey, Ahrda too edgy, Torin flexed his claws too often, Kiki bared his lips too wide. Small details which warned of danger and she met it, mastering the beasts as a matter of survival more than art. Quashing all trace of fear, feeding her anger so as to radiate an aura of seething rage and determination.

Even so she had to cut short the performance, giving the signal which brought the clowns running, tumbling, distracting attention while the handlers wafted tranquilizing vapors at the cats before guiding them from the ring. As they vanished from the area her cheeks burned to the yelled annoyance of the audience.

A hard crowd; mostly new arrivals and as yet uncalmed by the soothing atmosphere of Baatz. Rock-miners, mercenaries, hunters from nearby planets hungry for entertainment and free with lewd advice, suggestions, open invitations.

They quieted as the gymnasts began to spin in complex patterns of incredible dexterity; lithe bodies like living flames adorning the struts and poles with practiced grace.

"You were terrible." Old Valaban faced her in the tunnel beneath the stands. In the light from the ring his face was creased, worn, the livid scars which ran from scalp to chin on his left side a barred chiaroscuro. "An amateur couldn't have done worse and you know it. Hayter—"

"He's dead!"

"Sure—as you could have been a couple of times out there. But he died because of pride. You would have gone down because of stupidity."

She saw the change in his eyes and looked at her raised hand, loaded with the stock of her whip, heavy with its concealed blade.

"Sorry." He was a genius with animals and the claws which had ripped his face had paid the dues for a free tongue. "Val—I'm sorry."

"Something's wrong, girl. You should know what it is."

Tiredness. Turmoil—her brief sleep had been haunted by dreams. A face which dominated her universe. The glitter of a knife—the thought of what it would have felt like as it sheared home. At first nothing, the blade like a cat's claw too sharp to register. Then the sting, the burn, the horror of impending death.

The face—why couldn't she wash it from her mind?

Valaban said, "Women don't make good tamers as a rule. Nature's against them; at times their scent is too strong and makes the cats restless. You're lucky in that way but other things can be as bad as blood."

She said, curtly, "I'm not a fool. I bathe before each performance. I don't smell."

"But you sweat." He was blunt. "And I'm talking about scents, not smells. You're in rut," he accused. "A bitch in heat. I can't smell it but the animals can. They're males—do I have to spell it out?"

"You're sick! Perverted!"

"I'm alive." A hand rose to touch the scarred cheek. "I've had time to learn. To realize that you, me, all of us are just the same as any other animal. We all share the same hungers, the same fears. If you think you're special then you should quit the ring before it's too late. I'd hate to see your face look like mine."

He was trying to frighten her; such scars could be healed but he wore his like a badge. Would she have such courage? She knew the answer, knew too that such wounds would break her spirit. Even if the damaged tissue was repaired the trauma would remain and, once a tamer radiated fear, it was the end.

"Think about it," said Valaban. "I'll do what I can with the cats but the rest is up to you."

He vanished among the activity beneath the stands, Zucco taking his place. He was resplendent in his uniform; scarlet and gold flashing with scintillance. The king of a small world that he handled well.

He shook his head as he met her eyes. "Bad, Reiza—but you know that."

"It happens." She added, in an attempt to lessen her guilt, "The crowd didn't help."

"We've had worse. Maybe you should take a rest. Lacombe—"

"Isn't ready!" She was sharp in her rejection. Once let the man take her place and he would fight to keep it. "The cats would tear him apart."

"Maybe that's what they want." Zucco looked toward the mouth of the tunnel, the seats beyond, the faces blurred in the distance. "At least it would revive interest. We could do with something to fill the empty seats."

"The gate still falling?"

"Not fast, but falling. Well, it happens."

A tobey running out of tap. Soon would come the time to break up and move. To find another world and set down in another place. One which could only be more violent than Baatz.

And Dumarest?

"I told you, he's safe," snapped Zucco when she asked the question. "Why worry about him?"

"Is he still in the sump?"

"You know a better place?" He shrugged when she made no answer. "He'll keep. Just forget him. Now, as to your own problem, we'd better talk about it later." His head tilted as a roar came from the audience. "I'm due out there. Irina! Spall! Pryor! The rest of you! Stand ready!"

Fire-dancers assembled, almost nude, garish in paint and tinsel. On the ring flames would be leaping in a dancing pattern of red and gold, orange and scarlet. A furnace tinged with smoke into which the waiting dancers would throw themselves, merging with the searing fury, spinning, seeming to be burned to be reborn and rise again.

A spectacle to add to the rest. The life of the circus and one she had always enjoyed but now, oddly, she felt no elation. First Valaban and now Zucco. The first was genuinely concerned but the ringmaster would have his own motivations. Refused, he would turn ugly, promote Lacombe to her spot, find her a lesser place. Once she lost her status the descent would be inevitable. On another world she could have sold her skill to others but, on Baatz, that was impossible.

"No," she said. "By, God, no!"

A clown stared at her and moved quickly on. One she ignored as her hand closed on the stock of her whip. Zucco thought he held the master hand; her poor performance the weapon she had given him to justify any decision he might choose to make.

The victory in the war between them—one she determined he would never enjoy.

Dumarest stirred, feeling the sharp sting of teeth in his leg, seeing a small rodent dart away into the shadows. A scavenger of odorous waste and the creatures which fed on it. His blood and sweat had attracted it to a more wholesome feast.

He looked at his hand and the gemmed pin clutched in the fingers. His escape if he could use it, a weapon if he could not. If Ruval or Zucco came again to torture him he would not be so defenseless. One or both would lose an eye if not more.

He sat upright, fighting a wave of nausea. His mouth was dry and small tremors ran over his limbs. Bad but not as bad as he had been when shocked nerves and the beating made it impossible to stand or exercise control. Time in which he had drifted on the edges of oblivion wrapped in a red-shot nightmare of pain.

Now, ignoring the small shape which watched from the gloom, he bent over the manacle on his left wrist. A narrow band, closed tight, held by a simple lock. One into which he slipped the pin, moving it with practiced care as he searched for the tumbler. It slipped free and he drew in his breath with a sharp hiss before trying again. His hands were clumsy, quivering, the pin seeming to have a life of its own. At the third attempt it held and he applied pressure, easing it as the slender probe bent, trying to hit a workable compromise. Too much force and the metal could snap, too little and it wouldn't throw the tumbler. Sweat stung his eyes before the catch yielded with a click.

The other followed and Dumarest stretched his arms to ease

the ache in his shoulders. The belt still held him chained to the wall but it too yielded to the pin. A few moments and he stood upright, breathing deeply as the released circlet fell to clash against the wall.

A sound which produced echoes; small scurryings in the dimness, vibrations which quivered and died as he stepped toward the door to his right. One Zucco had used and Ruval after him but it was locked as was another facing it. Strong catches against which the pin was useless and he slipped it into his hair as he turned to study the pounding machine.

It held a pulse like that of a heart; an irregular throbbing as it churned the detritus from above and fed it into the pipe. Masses fed from a hopper yielding its contents when full. Accompanied with water so as to make a liquid sludge. If he could open the pipe it offered a chance of escape.

If he could breathe while traveling along it. If he didn't get jammed in a bend. If he didn't drown in the filth of the lagoon into which it emptied.

A gamble he couldn't take; the room was devoid of tools, the pipe impossible to open.

Back at the door Zucco had used he examined the hinges then tensed, ear to the panel. A moment and he backed, flattening himself against the wall, the gemmed pin gripped sword-fashion in his right hand.

The door opened and Reiza stepped into the sump.

"Earl? Earl Dumarest?" She spun as he stepped behind her, flattening his shoulders against the thrown-back panel of the door. "My God!" Her eyes widened as she looked at him. "What the hell have they done to you?"

"They?"

"You don't think I had anything to do with this." She looked at the blood on his face, the blotches on his body. "The swine! I should have guessed."

She wore a robe of blue touched with silver. This she untied and slipped from her shoulders to reveal the white nudity of her body, loins and breasts embraced by silver lace.

"Here." She handed him the robe. "Put this on and let's get out of here. It stinks!"

Dumarest said, "Is anyone out there? Ruval? Anyone?"

"No." Her nose wrinkled again. "Hurry up and put on that robe. You need a bath."

It was scented, warm, a place of luxury in which to wallow as the dirt and smell was washed away. More water replaced the soiled and he felt the sting of medications and the easing of strained muscles. Tissues knotted by the charge of the wand but the red mesh of broken capillaries remained together with the purple of ugly bruises.

"They'll go," said Reiza. She stood beside the bath, her skin dewed with condensed vapor. "I've got a salve which will help. Something for your eyes, too."

They were puffed, swollen from the impact of Ruval's fists as his ribs ached from the impact of his boot. Pain caused by cracked bone but the toe had slipped to prevent more serious damage. Dumarest sat as the woman checked his torso with surprisingly strong fingers.

"This will hurt a little." She reached for a syringe from among a litter held in a wooden box bearing a name burned in the lid. Valaban's kit, the contents more suited to the treatment of animals than men. "Hold still, now."

A hypogun would have been more efficient but the needle was sharp enough and the hormone-enriched bone glue better than bandages.

As she finished Dumarest said, "You've done this before."

"On animals, yes."

"And men?"

She straightened without answering to stand before him, hands on hips, legs straddled. In the glow of the lamp her skin held a nacreous sheen, small gleams coming from the silver lace marring her nudity. A woman displaying herself and Dumarest looked at the long columns of her thighs, the swell of hips, the narrow waist, the contours of her breasts. The body of a magnificent animal and one matched by the face.

She said, bluntly, "If you like what you see it's yours."

"Just like that?"

"For me, yes." Her breath came faster as she stared at his own nudity. "It happens and no one knows just how or why. A person in a crowd, a single glance, and it's done. A need. An obsession. Call it love or madness it's just the same. You've got to have that person. For me it happened with you."

"Is that why you came to rescue me?"

"No." She was blunt in her honesty. "You were in my mind—I can't deny that, but I had another reason. I still have it. "Zucco—" She broke off, looking at his face. "You know Zucco?"

Dumarest nodded.

"He wants to use me, degrade me, but I'm damned if I'm going to let him do it. You can give me something to use against him."

"Such as?"

"Melome. You know her. You asked after her. Why?"

He said, dryly, "That's what Zucco wanted to know."

"But you didn't tell him. You—" She broke off as she realized what he was thinking. "No, Earl! No! It isn't like that. I'm not working with Zucco. I didn't rescue you just to gain your trust. Please! You've got to believe that!"

An easy path to take but his caution warned him against it. The rescue, the bribe of her body, the relaxing waters of the bath—all could be the steps of a master plan.

He said, "Zucco is the ringmaster. Surely he would know why Melome was bought."

"Not necessarily. Shakira has his own methods. A lot goes on which only he knows about."

"Shakira?"

"The owner of the circus." She handed Dumarest a pot containing a clear jelly. "Use this salve. Rub it in all over. The gymnasts use it and it works." Her eyes lingered on his face before she turned away. "I'd better get dressed and find you something to wear."

The salve stung a little, the momentary discomfort yielding to a warm glow as it dried. Alone Dumarest examined the chamber, the bed, the few furnishings it contained. A cabinet held costumes and other garments; mementoes of earlier roles of those used in different performances. Like all circus-folk on the way up Reiza would have had to be versatile. A shelf held packages of cosmetics, threads, sequins, a photograph edged in black. One of a man.

He smiled as Dumarest picked up the portrait, the surface shimmering to give an illusion of life. As the warmth of his hand triggered the cycle, Dumarest heard the whisper of a low, intimate voice.

"I love you. My darling, I love you. Reiza, my dearest, always be mine. I love you. I . . ."

The voice ended as Dumarest replaced the photograph and continued his examination.

A table bore a glowing lamp, a shelf beneath it the weight of a decanter and goblets. The bed was covered with an ornate creation of fine threads woven on silk; pictures depicting dragons, felines, couples in exotic embraces. A rack held books. A vase a cluster of crystalline flowers.

A small place, cramped by necessity, a box which held the appurtenances of a life. One which held the sense of lonely isolation.

The bath lay in an adjoining chamber, the tub still half-full of water. A curtain, now drawn back, closed the opening. A whip lay coiled on a second chair. The gemmed pin he had used to free himself lay beside the lamp. The door leading to the passage outside was masked by a curtain of vividly colored plastic tubes and balls threaded on strings ending in copper bells.

Dumarest heard their chime as Ruval thrust his way into the room.

CHAPTER FIVE

He was dressed as Dumarest remembered, a tear now in the blouse where the pin had been, a white patch of bandage resting over one eye. Halting, he stared, air rasping through his nostrils as he drew in his breath.

Dumarest said, "You've come for the money. Good. Give me pen and paper and I'll write that note."

Words which could have been silence for all the notice the big man took.

"You," he said. "I guessed that bitch might have you here. Sneaked down and let you out, did she? And I might never have known if I hadn't missed my pin." His eyes moved to where it lay. "So you found it. Maybe took it during the fight. Well, no matter. I'll take you back now."

"No," said Dumarest.

"You going to stop me?" Ruval smiled as he looked at Dumarest's naked body, his empty hands. "No knife now, friend."

"No knife," agreed Dumarest. "But I've got your pin. You want it?" He moved forward, snatched it up, threw it. "Here."

Ruval was fast, batting at the spinning glitter arcing toward his eyes, sending it to fall to one side. A distraction he had mistaken for an attack and Dumarest had reached him before the bauble had fallen, left hand sending stiffened fingers jabbing at the face, right hand rising, the heel of the palm forward, slashing upwards at the nose as the big man threw back his head.

A blow which would have killed had it landed, shattering the

59

nasal septum and sending splinters of bone up into the sinus cavities and the brain.

But it missed as Ruval twisted his head, landing instead on the cheek, creating surface bruising and internal damage.

Ruval snarled, twisting away, his foot rising to lash out in a savage kick. Dumarest dodged, felt the brush of the boot against his knee, dodged again as the big man sent a fist at his stomach. A hard and vicious fighter careless if he killed or maimed so long as he won. One now maddened with rage.

"You scum! Making a mock of me! Laughing at me! I'll make you laugh—the next time you go into the sump it'll be as garbage!"

Talk wasted energy but the big man could spare it as he could the wild blows which ruptured air. Strength Dumarest lacked; weakened by his ordeal he knew the fight had to be ended soon or he would go down.

He weaved to one side, his left arm stabbing, the fingers like a blunted spear as they thrust into the fat and muscle over Ruval's heart. A blow followed by the edge of his right palm slashing lower down and to the side. As it hit his knee jerked up toward the groin as he jerked his head forward to slam his skull against the other's nose.

Ruval cried out, staggering backward, blood from his broken nose masking his mouth and chin. Minor damage; his massive bulk had protected his internal organs and Dumarest had missed the small target of the genitals. He backed to gain room to maneuver; his speed would be useless once clutched in Ruval's crushing grip.

"Now!" The big man wiped a hand across his face smearing its back with vivid carmine. "Now, you scum!"

He came in a rush; a living mass of bone and muscle, powered by hate. A killing machine intent on destruction. Dumarest sprang toward the adjoining chamber, felt his foot turn beneath him, staggered and, before he could regain his balance, Ruval was on him.

Dumarest felt the pound of a fist against his cheek, another at his jaw—and gagged as a third found his throat.

A blow to the larynx which blossomed into searing agony filled his mouth with the taste of blood, blocking the passage of air to his lungs. A killing blow—unable to breathe—death was scant minutes away.

He dived within the circle of Ruval's arms, his own lifting, elbows spread to keep the other's hands from his eyes. His own darted toward the thick neck, thumbs searching for the carotid arteries pulsing beneath the surface. Finding them. Closing them with pressure to cut off the supply of blood to the brain.

Waiting, fighting to remain calm, to maintain the pressure until Ruval sagged and he slumped unconscious. Falling toward the bath as Dumarest released his hold, splashing into it and coming to rest face-down in the water.

Dumarest left him there. He was dying, blackness edging his vision as he lurched toward the whip now lying on the floor. A twist and the blade came free of the stock; twelve inches of flattened steel, pointed, edged to a third of its length. Bells jangled as he tore down the masking curtain, slashing a strand free, catching one of the thin plastic tubes.

Tilting back his head he drove the blade into his throat.

A calculated thrust; the point guided by the fingers of his left hand, piercing the trachea just above the breastbone and well below the larynx. A stab which opened the windpipe between two ridges of cartilage, the cut widening to the drag of the blade. As it came free Dumarest forced the plastic tube into the opening.

And breathed.

Falling to his knees in a welling darkness as he sucked air through the narrow tube; the entire universe diminished to the stream of oxygen which was his life.

After the fifth blatant error Valaban snapped, "Get hold of yourself, Reiza. You're confusing the beasts. Keep on like this and you'll make them useless. Lose your reputation too, but that's your business. The animals are mine."

"You tend them—I work them!"

"Then do it. Damn it, I've seen tyros do better!"

A harsh rebuke but she deserved it and Valaban knew his trade. As she knew hers too well not to know he was right.

More softly he said, "Get a shower. Some sleep. Go into town for a while. Give the cats a rest until you've settled down. You know what I mean."

Good advice but even if she took it the torment of waiting would still remain. Irritably she strode from the ring, seeing Zucco standing in the passage, his normal finery subdued under a cloak of black trimmed with yellow. A means to remain inconspicuous in the shadows? A possibility and if true meant that he had been watching her. More ammunition to feed his intentions, but now she had weapons of her own.

"Reiza!" He fell into step beside her. "You have my sympathy. It was a dreadful thing to have happened. You were lucky Dumarest didn't hurt you."

He knew—there was little that went on he didn't know about, but some things had to remain speculation. Now it suited her to be ignorant.

"Dumarest?"

"A murderer. I sensed it from the first. Now we have proof."

"Ruval? He drowned in my bath."

"With bruises on his face and throat. We know who must have put them there. Dumarest—"

She halted and turned to face him, her eyes matching the hardness of her voice.

"Yes, Dumarest. The man you gassed then stripped and chained in the sump. One you tortured and Ruval must have helped. Well, Ruval has paid. It could be your turn soon, Jac."

"You think he could beat me?" His amusement was genuine. "That scum? Have you forgotten what I was before I became ringmaster?" Abruptly he smiled. "We quarrel for no purpose. You have chosen to care for Dumarest as another would care for a sick dog. A weakness I deplore but I am willing to let you indulge yourself. Simply be aware of what he is. A liar. A cheat. A thief. A murderer."

"A man!"

One such as Zucco could never be. His strength was built on the weakness of others, his power the fruit of pandering to decadent tastes.

He said, quietly, "A man who will use you as he used Helga. I suggest you remember that, my dear. And, when you are sane again, I shall be waiting."

Smoothness coupled with the vicious barb of a subtle tongue. Why else mention Helga if not to make her jealous? And why no mention of what must have been foremost in his mind? The details Dumarest could have told her about Melome and which he had wanted so desperately to know? And why had he made no move against Dumarest?

The answer waited in the infirmary where the doctor greeted her with a smile.

"He's fine." He answered her question before she could ask it, jerking his head toward where Dumarest sat in a chair sipping from a beaker. "Basic laced with brandy from Shakira's own store. His orders. All to be of the best."

"He knows?"

"Of course. I sent him a full report. We don't get many patients who've given themselves a tracheotomy. A good one too, I must admit, but he almost left it too late. Of course there was other damage; the larynx, cellular disruption, dehydration, nervous degeneration—used to excess those wands can be nasty things. The gas didn't help either."

'But he's all right now?'

"Fine."

Healed by the drugs and skill of the doctor, the magic of slowtime. Dressed now in a drab robe of dull puce which was a little too short for his height. He smiled as she came toward him.

"My lady, it seems I must thank you for my life."

The formality stunned her then she understood; such a man would be accustomed to moving among those to whom procedure was paramount. To be less than punctilious would be to invite retribution.

She said, "This is the circus, Earl. We're ordinary people. You don't have to crawl on your knees."

"Ordinary?" His eyes studied her, bringing a flush of pleasure to her cheeks. "Whatever you are, Reiza, you're not that. And you did save me."

"I found you," she corrected. "But you'd already saved yourself. Unconscious but breathing steady. We've just patched you up and speeded the healing. Now, I'll bet you're hungry." She saw him glance at the empty beaker which had held a fluid rich in protein, sickly with glucose, laced with vitamins. And Shakira's brandy—that had been an extra. "For real food; meat and richness and things you can get your teeth into. Come on—I'm buying." To the doctor she said, "Can't you find him something more decent to wear?"

Dumarest said, "Where are my own clothes?"

"God knows—we'll find them later. Please, Doc, can't you hurry?"

He produced pants and a blouse in faded blue together with soft shoes tied with thin laces. The legacy of a dead man, perhaps, but they fitted well enough and Reiza was satisfied. Delaying only long enough to change from her costume into a gown of lilac ornamented with jet she led the way to the outer galleries, to a restaurant Dumarest had used before.

"The best," she said. "You'll like it here. Voe!" She saw the waiter's glance of recognition as he approached her companion. "You order, Earl." She added, with a touch of malice, "Let's have the same meal you had before."

"No. This should be special."

"True." She was glad he hadn't tried to dissemble. "The best, Voe. Red meat and all the trimmings. Some wine too—this is a celebration!"

But it was shared with an invisible companion. Had Helga used this very glass? Sat at this very table? Seen his smile as he looked at her? Felt the same acceleration of her heart?

Foolishness and she knew it. Knew too that she was talking too fast and laughing too loud. Eating too little and drinking too much.

As she reached for the decanter Dumarest leaned forward and caught her hand.

"It's none of my business," he said. "You can drink yourself stupid if you want. I've no right to interfere. But do it for the right reasons."

"Such as?"

"That's for you to decide. Most do it for escape. Is there anything you need to run from?"

"No."

"Zucco?"

"No. I—" She shook her head and lifted the decanter as he released her hand. Wine filled her glass in a ruby stream. Looking at it she said, "I guess I'm running away from myself. Have you ever wanted to run?"

"Often."

"I find that hard to believe."

"It's the truth." Dumarest helped himself to some of the wine. Scarlet, the hue of a cyber's robe, the Cyclan which hunted him from world to world. "Were you born in the circus?"

"No. I was sold. Twenty years ago now when I was ten. On Tsopei."

"A harsh world."

"You know it?"

"I've heard of it."

"If you're smart you'll leave it at that." She was bitter. "If there are worse places I've yet to find them. Burn during the day, freeze at night, fighting insects, rot, mildew and, if you don't eat what walks, crawls or flies they'll eat you. Like they did my parents. My kin.''

"It happens."

"Too often," she agreed. "But I guess I was lucky. The man who took me in intended me for something else but an agent of the circus landed and offered a good price. I guess he could see more than others. He had me taught, trained, and—well, that's about it." She swallowed some of her wine. "And you, Earl?"

"Much the same as yourself. I ran away."

"From home? Your world? Which was it?" She frowned at his answer. "Earth? That's an odd name. I've never heard of it. And now?"

"I move around."

"Just that? Don't you do anything else?"

Managing to stay alive. Dodging the hunters. Searching for clues which would guide him back home. Things he left unsaid.

"I'm looking."

"For what? Happiness?" She shrugged as she lifted her glass. "Isn't that what we're all doing? Hoping to find that elusive something which will make everything wonderful? Sometimes you think you've found it then, when you feel most secure, everything falls apart." As it had when Hayter had died. As it threatened to do now—why was he so cold? "Earl!"

Dumarest said, "I haven't forgotten what you said before Ruval attacked."

"Then—"

"I'm honored. More than that—overwhelmed." He paused, sensing her inner turmoil, conscious of the danger it created. A proud woman who, rejected, could become a vicious enemy. The only ally he had in the world of the circus and even now he wasn't sure if she worked for Zucco or not. "Reiza, I—"

"Don't say it!" Wine slopped over her hand to stain the cloth with the color of blood. "If it's a rejection I don't want to hear it. Just get up and leave."

Her, the table, the circus, Melome, his chance of finding Earth.

Dumarest said, "When I leave we go together. I was going to suggest we do it now."

"Earl!" Happiness sparkled in her eyes. "Earl, darling, you—" She broke off, frowning as a man halted at the table. He held a parcel and wore a sigil on his blouse. The mark of Chen Wei. "What do you want?"

"The man." He looked at Dumarest. "You are to accompany me at once to the office of Tayu Shakira."

It was a place filled with an indefinable scent which hung like a ghostly emanation in the air. One composed of subtle spices, of flavors, smokes, blooms, the taint of flesh, the hint of seas. The perfume of a thousand worlds which the circus had known inhaled by the man who sat behind a wide desk. He gestured toward a chair and waited until Dumarest had seated himself and the guide had left them alone.

"You are well, I trust?"

"Well."

"And comfortable?"

"Very."

The truth; the parcel the guide had carried had contained his clothes, refurbished and as good as new. Only the knife had been missing and, as he watched, Shakira lifted it from somewhere behind the desk and set it down before him.

"A fine blade," he said. "One worth studying."

As he was himself and Dumarest, ignoring the knife, searched the man with his eyes.

Tall, slender, a skull topped with raven hair sweeping back from a point between and above the eyes. High brows sheltered deep-set orbs in slanted sockets. The nose was thin, predatory, the mouth a gash. The skin, olive, held a mesh of tiny lines which added to the mask-like appearance of the face.

"You are a fighter," he said. "And have used this knife to kill. Often?"

"Only when necessary."

"Of course." A thin hand reached from the wide sleeve of a blouse marked with an arabesque of gold on a background of lavender. "And yet you drew it here in the circus. An unusual thing to happen on Baatz where violence is rare."

Dumarest said, dryly, "My experiences hardly justify that statement."

"You miss the point. The air within the circus is filtered and those who work here are sheltered from the enervating influence of the outside atmosphere. Visitors carry their apathy with them. You did not. Either you are proof against the external vapors or are able to rise above their influence. I suspect the latter. Tell me, now, and be honest. Have you made no errors since landing?"

Too many and Dumarest admitted it.

"Good." Shakira was pleased. "If you had been immune it would have proved nothing. As it is you have adapted to a potentially dangerous environment. Dangerous for you, that is, and for all who have enemies. Think of a snake," he urged. "A master of movement over sand and rock. But set it on a sheet of oiled glass and it is helpless. It can only writhe and squirm, easy prey for any predator. So, for a while on this world, you were at a disadvantage. Here!" The knife spun glittering through the air. Dumarest caught it an inch from his face. "Fast too," mused Shakira. "The reports did not lie."

"Reports from whom?"

"Those who need to make them." Shakira dismissed the subject with a small gesture. "There are questions you wish to ask?"

Only one of importance but if the owner knew as much as he claimed then he would know of Dumarest's interest in Melome. He hadn't mentioned that and subtlety was a game two could play.

Dumarest said, casually, "I'm surprised the circus is so large. I wouldn't have thought Baatz capable of supporting it. But I guess you rely on the concessions."

"You've worked in circuses?"

"Carnivals."

"It is not the same."

"Maybe not," agreed Dumarest. "But I've never known a circus which doesn't have sideshows. Basically it's all the same. When you come down to it what else is a circus but entertainment? So, logically, everything goes. It all belongs."

"Not in the circus of Chen Wei."

"But—"

"We move," said Shakira. "We travel from world to world and with us, like those small limpets which cling to the leviathans of the deep oceans, come the purveyors of common entertainment. They are mere appendages—if lost the circus would not suffer."

"And the circus itself?"

"A compilation of the unusual. Of the rare and particular. The ordinary has no place among us. Each represents the apex of his art."

Dumarest said, "Like Zucco?"

"He has his skills."

"I think I can guess what they are. And you?"

"I have my talent. I have it as you have it as every living

67

creature has it. That special attribute which sets it above its fellows. The ability to sing sweeter, run faster, see more clearly, swim farther, dive deeper, kill faster—always there is something. Usually it is a small advantage and one negated when set against a greater development but, always, it is there. Here, in the circus, are those who have learned what they are good at and have excelled beyond all others in doing it. Others have yet to train and develop their skills; buds swelling toward full bloom. As for myself?" Shakira made a small gesture. "My skill lies in recognizing the potential of others. Your own, for example."

"You flatter me."

"That would be stupid. It would be even more stupid to refuse to recognize the obvious. It is a mistake I never make." Again Shakira made the small gesture, lifting both hands in an upward movement. "You have more questions?"

"One." It was time to get to the point; the gesture had held connotations of dismissal and he was tired of the fencing. Dumarest said, flatly, "How much for Melome?"

"So we come to it—the girl."

"As you've known all along. I want her."

"So it would seem." Shakira's thin lips formed a smile. "Enough to break into my circus, hurt one of my people, threaten another, kill a third—"

"In self-defense."

"True, and Ruval deserved all that happened to him. But the rest?"

"I came for Melome."

"You say that as if it gives you justification for all you did," mused Shakira. "Had you forgotten she is mine?"

"No."

"But it didn't matter, is that it? You would have willingly stolen the girl."

"I wanted what I had paid for. A deal had been arranged and money paid in advance as a token of good faith."

"Fifty kobolds," agreed Shakira. "It was that which decided my agent to act. Too often things of value are lost because of delay and he knew I would not be gentle had he failed. Kalama cheated you. Be thankful it was not for more."

"To hell with the money!" Dumarest fought to remain calm. He found it hard. The air held the traces of too many distant worlds, Shakira himself too like a serpent in his subtle deviations.

A man enjoying the situation. Yet here he was the master and he had the girl. "How much for Melome?"

"Would you be willing to pay a hundred thousand kobolds?" Shakira lifted his hands as Dumarest made no answer. "A ridiculous sum, I agree, but you don't really want to buy the girl. Think of the problems owning her would create. Let us decide on a price, then, for your original agreement."

"That was done."

"But I own the girl now and my values are not the same as Kalama's. There are only two things you could give me which I don't already own. One is your skill. The other is the knowledge you carry in your brain. The skill can be purchased but the knowledge must be freely given." Shakira's voice hardened a little. "Why do want to use the girl?"

"You know what she does."

"Of course, but few willingly seek the terror she induces. Some men will do it once for an act of bravado but rarely twice. Yet you wanted more and more of her song. The action of a desperate man or a stupid one as was your later pursuit. I do not think you to be stupid and am curious as to why you are so desperate. So willing to risk your life to get the girl."

"There is something I want and she can help me to find it." It was not enough and Dumarest knew it. Bluntly he added more. "She can help me find my way home to Earth."

"Earth?" A veil filmed Shakira's eyes. "You believe in legends?"

"Earth is no legend."

"And you claim it as your home world. I find that interesting. We must discuss it in greater detail." Shakira rose from his chair. He was taller than Dumarest had estimated, the golden arabesque of his blouse continued over the pants of matching color, the garments blending so that he seemed to be a creature of lavender laced with gold. "But later. Now we must settle the question of price."

"I offer to share my knowledge."

"Which will be valuable, true, but it isn't enough. You could learn nothing and how would I profit? I want your skill. You must agree to work for me." Shakira added, "If you want the girl, my friend, you have no choice."

CHAPTER SIX

———••———

Melome had changed. The waif of the market with the dirt and thinness and ghastly pallor had gone as had the ragged clothing, the belt holding the reeled spools, the lank straggle of the hair. Instead Dumarest looked at a pubescent girl dressed in a neatly belted gown, the long hair braided and set in shimmering coils, the nails trimmed and polished. When she smiled she held the glow of inner health.

A miracle wrought with expensive and intensive therapy, but some of the earlier traces remained; the almost luminous waxen appearance of the skin, the bruised and haunted eyes. Windows which held secrets, unchanging as she lifted her hands, a strand of woven metal between them, as bright and coldly gleaming as her hair.

"Touch it," said Shakira. "Sit and hold the metal."

The contact which would open the door to the past.

Dumarest sat, cross-legged, the metal pliant and cool in his hands. The strand was long, reaching in a double line halfway across the chamber to where Melome now stood against a wall. At Shakira's touch an instrument came to life filling the air with the wail of pipes and the throb of a drum.

Music recorded, refined, filling the room with a relentless pulsing. Closing around Dumarest, enfolding him in a web of silence broken only by the throbbing beat, the nerve-scratching wail, rising, demanding—

The ship!

71

He must concentrate on the ship. The cabin. The precious book.

The book!

Melome began to sing.

Sound which dominated, directed, engrossed—and became a scream of rage.

"You bastard! You've been stealing again!"

"No!" Dumarest cringed, backing away, sick with the terror which knotted his stomach. Vomiting the scrap of food he'd taken from the pot, the first in two days. "No! Please, no!"

The lash of a belt and pain to add to his fear. Another and the heavy buckle tore at flesh, breaking the skin, sending blood to mingle with the dirt coating his buttocks and legs. The single garment he wore ripped as a hand snatched at his shoulder, the belt lashing at his nakedness, beating him down to the tamped dirt of the floor, sending him in a foetal huddle.

A child of eight years terrified for his life.

"Bastard!" The man, drunk, gloated in his sadistic pleasure. "You no-good bastard! Eat without asking my permission, eh? Stuffing your guts without getting my say-so. I'll teach you. By, God, I'll teach you!"

With the belt, his hands, boots, charred sticks from the fire. Augmenting the hell of normal existence into a dimension of screaming terror. Standing now, beating, beating, beating until his arm grew tired. Staggering away at last to gulp raw liquor from a bottle, spitting a mouthful into the fire. In the sudden flame his shadow loomed against a wall like a grotesque creature from nightmare.

One which blurred to become a girl with braided, silver hair.

"Earl?" Shakira was at his side. "Here."

The wine was rich, pungent, held in a goblet of hammered brass. A warmth which eased his throat and comforted his stomach. Dumarest swallowed it all; if Shakira intended harm he'd had time enough to have done it by now.

Sitting, he looked at the metallic strand, now lying in a loop before him. The goblet held decorations of men and beasts chasing each other in an eternal circle. The carpet was woven from fine materials in a blend of barred and chevron designs. The light came from an overhead dome as if from a luminous pearl.

Things noted with a strange detachment while, deep inside of him, terror remained.

Keil, the man had been Keil, one of a succession who had governed his formative years. Beasts shaped like men lacking any generosity, charity or understanding. Using him for the labor he could provide. Working him like an animal as they worked their women. Lusting in violence and the dealing of pain.

"Earl?" Shakira again, his face close, eyes bright and questing. "Tell me, quickly before the impression fades. Was it stronger than before?"

Too strong—such terror should remain buried.

"Her talent is unimpaired." Shakira beamed at Dumarest's nod. "I had fears it might have diminished. Too often sensitives seem only to work their best when subjected to physical hardship but this does not seem to be the case with Melome. And the intensity? The detail? How was that?"

"Clear." Dumarest held out the goblet for more wine. "Too damned clear."

The beating could have been a second ago—his body burned from recollected blows. He could smell the dirt, the vomit, his own excreta and sweat. Taste the blood from his bitten lips, the acid bile of cringing terror.

Terror!

Her song was well-named.

"It could be a matter of sharpened ability or one of concentration," mused Shakira. "In the market she was dull, spiritless, the effort must have drained her vital energies. Now, rested, she is reenergized. Couple this with the fact you are alone—but, no. I doubt it. Does a fire care how many warm themselves at its blaze? The song induces a reaction in those in contact. One or more it could be the same. And yet?" He broke off, thinking.

Dumarest said, "I failed. I missed my target."

"By much?"

Minutes would have been too much but he had missed by years. Her strengthened ability? His own lack of concentration? What must he do to ensure success?

He said, "I want to try again. Now."

"It would not be wise."

"I'll be the judge of that." Dumarest reached for the metal strand, looked up as Shakira kicked it beyond his reach. "We have an agreement."

"That you work for me until such time as you have gained what you want from Melome. An unfair bargain; you could have achieved success at your very first try. But I accepted the gamble and you must do the same.''

''Must?''

''You have no choice.'' Shakira lifted his hands as if demanding attention. ''I mean that quite literally. To think that you could use violence against me would be madness. To try it would be to commit suicide. You could leave now and I will stand the loss. A broken agreement—these things happen and the fault would be mine for having misjudged you. But stay and you will have no further option. You will do what I command when I command it. To work for me is to obey.''

To be beaten, burned, starved, made to grovel, to beg—the memory of the past was too recent. As was the lesson it had taught. To yield was to die and to do it slowly. And Dumarest was no longer an eight-year-old tormented child.

''Earl!'' Shakira stepped back as Dumarest rose to his feet, reading the emotions he saw, recognizing the determination. ''Think, man! Attack me and you die!''

''Perhaps.'' Dumarest took one step closer. ''But you will go first.''

''Wait!'' The thin hands lifted in a gesture of defense or warning. ''You are disturbed. Affected by your recent experience. I should have remembered that. Remembered, too, that you are no ordinary man. You have heard of the Band of Obedience?''

''A slave-collar, you mean?''

''The name is unimportant; they are the same. A circlet which is locked around the neck. It contains a device which can be activated from a distance to cause excruciating pain leading to death. It also contains explosives which can be detonated. That same charge will blow if the collar is cut or the lock tampered with. A barbaric device but one which has its uses. Refined it can be most useful.''

''To persuade others to keep agreements?''

''Exactly.'' Shakira lowered his hands. ''While you were being treated in the infirmary I thought it best to take certain precautions. Leave now and they will be negated. Stay and you will obey me—or die!''

Reiza stirred, mumbling in sleepy contentment, pressing herself against Dumarest like a kitten seeking warmth. A woman who moved her arm to hold him close while whispering in half-wakeful awareness.

"Earl, my darling. You've made me so happy. I love you. I shall love you forever."

This he doubted; passion swift to bloom could fade as quickly.

"Earl?"

She sighed as he stroked her hair, lapsing again into sleep as he stared at the ceiling of her chamber. One adorned with lacelike traceries, black against the nacreous glow shining through the plastic membrane. Artificial moonlight which dimly revealed the furnishings of the room, the mane of her hair, the stark whiteness of her naked arms and shoulders. Against it the traceries took on shape and form.

Bars illustrating the trap he was in.

One baited by Melome.

Shakira's property now and his price had been high. Dumarest's hand rose to his neck as he remembered the weight of the slave-collar he had worn on a world far distant. One he had managed to shed but that had been obvious and Shakira's threat was not.

A bluff?

A possibility and Dumarest considered it as his fingers probed at his neck. They found no lumps or foreign masses but that meant little; a capsule could have been implanted within an inner organ or a time-poison administered. There were a score of ways it could have been done by those skilled in the ways of death.

And, to be sure Shakira was bluffing, he had first to know the man.

He grew on the traceries as Dumarest painted a mental picture of the head, the body, the face, the hands. These details held a subtle oddness as did his clothing, his very walk. A glide rather than punctuated steps which together with the arabesque markings over the matching pants and blouse gave the man an ophidian appearance. A snakelike resemblance accentuated by the slant of the eyes, the thin mask of the face. Yet the hands did not match and he remembered the lifting gesture. One of dismissal, then of defense and warning. Again as a shrug but, always, the same double lift of both appendages. An idiosyncrasy which could mean nothing like the rest of the details; to know the man he must learn more.

"Earl?" Reiza stirred under his hand. "Darling, you want—"

"To talk," he said. "Wake up."

"Talk?" She laughed and pressed herself closer to him.

"Darling, you must be joking." Then, as she saw his face with clearer eyes, she said, "You mean it. You really mean it!"

"Tell me about Shakira. What do you know about him?"

"Not much." She reared upright, white in the dim glow, the mounds of her breasts tipped with areolas of darkness. "He owns the circus and gives the orders. If you're wondering about the name forget it. The circus of Chen Wei has existed for over a hundred years. It has a good reputation and I guess Shakira thought it worth keeping."

Profit before pride. Dumarest said, "Did you ever meet the previous owner? No?" Which meant Shakira had run the circus for at least twenty years. "Has anyone?"

"Valaban, maybe. He handles the beasts. You've met him." On the tour of inspection Shakira had insisted he take with Reiza as his guide. "He might know. I'll ask him."

"Anyone else?" Then, as she hesitated, Dumarest said, "Never mind. I'll find out for myself. But about Shakira. Have you ever crossed him or know of anyone who has?"

"What are you getting at, Earl?"

"I need to know."

"And don't intend saying for why." Reiza fell silent then, with an abrupt movement, rose from the bed, standing naked as if a statue carved from alabaster before slipping on a robe. "I thought we'd grown close enough for me to be trusted."

"I trust you."

"Then—"

"I want facts," he said. "Small things, maybe, but enough to build the picture of a man. If you don't want to cooperate then I'll find out some other way but I'd rather not attract his attention." He paused for a moment then added, "When we first met he hinted that he wasn't gentle with those who failed him. True?"

"Are you in trouble, Earl?"

"I could be."

"And you want my help, is that it?" She smiled at his nod. "Well, it isn't much. Shakira's a hard man. A cold one and, yes, he isn't gentle with those who fail him. Do your best and he'll be fair even though he may want your best to be always better. Slack and he comes down hard. Keep slacking and you're out."

She was talking from the viewpoint of an artiste; her opinion conditioned by her work. Dumarest wanted finer data.

"Do you know of anyone who defied him and got away with it?"

"No. Zucco likes to give the impression he had but he's lying. He might act the boss but Shakira is the one who cracks the whip. When they are together there is no doubt who is the real master."

"What does he eat?"

"What?"

Dumarest was patient. "What kind of food does Shakira eat? How often? Does he have any unusual habits? Any personal dislikes? Things like colors," he explained. "Loud noises. Certain kinds of music. Smells. Does he play cards? Gamble? Encourage others to take risks? Has he ever struck anyone? Lost his temper in public? Is he easily amused? Does he—"

"No," said Reiza. "He isn't amused, I mean. I've never seen him appear happy. Even when he smiles it's more like a grimace and I've never heard him laugh. As for the rest—" She shrugged. "I don't know," she admitted. "When young I was too busy working to take any notice and, later, well minding your own business gets to be a habit. I've no time for gossip and rumor."

Two things which would have helped the most.

Dumarest said, "When you guided me around there was a part of the circus we didn't enter."

"Shakira's private quarters," she explained. "They're strictly out of bounds."

"To everyone? Cleaners? Servants?"

"Everyone." She frowned. "At least that's what I thought. Come to think of it someone has to do the cleaning."

And someone had to take care of the other sensitives. There had to be others; why else had Shakira bought Melome if not to add to his collection? But why did he want such a collection at all? Circuses were for the display of trained animals and skilled people before a large audience. Sensitives were unable to entertain more than a few at a time and, like physical freaks, their attraction was limited. An expensive luxury—and a man who retained the old name of the circus because of profit would not waste money.

"Earl?"

"A moment, Reiza."

He wanted to look at the pattern from a different viewpoint and, suddenly, the pieces fell into place. If Melome was alone then she must have been set as a lure; one he could never resist.

Following her he had walked into the trap and now it had snapped tight around him.

Did Shakira know the value of what he held?

If so he had been cunning even to the extent of offering a free choice. Dumarest wondered what would have happened had he decided to leave. An academic point now and he wasted no time considering it. Set against what he hoped to learn from Melome the risk had been acceptable. A gamble that Shakira was what he seemed and would keep his word. That his threat had been a bluff. That the luck which had turned sour would become sweet again.

"Earl!" Reiza was impatient. "What's the matter with you? You wake me up, get me to talk, then forget I'm alive."

"Sorry." Dumarest lifted himself in the bed. "I was thinking."

"About us?"

"Of course."

"Of our future together?" A smile banished the last of her irritation. "Darling, why didn't you say? What had you in mind? Shall—no!" She snapped her fingers. "Why guess when there's no need? Krystyna can tell us."

From somewhere came a low snuffling, the sound of a laugh quickly suppressed, a rumble which could have been a snore. Sounds Reiza ignored as she led the way through narrow passages flanked with doors. Living quarters little better than cubicles but cheap and acceptable to those inside.

"She's good, Earl. Really good. She even foretold the way Hayter would die. I didn't believe her then and now I wish I had. Not that it would have made any difference."

Dumarest remembered the talking photograph.

"You were close?"

"Hayter and I? Yes." Her tone ended the subject. "I saw her again recently. I was having some trouble with my act and she gave me some good advice. She even mentioned a stranger coming into my life. It must have been you, Earl. If nothing else I owe her for that."

The weakness of her kind; to confuse prediction with performance. A trait of all who were superstitious and those who lived on the razor-edge of danger were always prone to become that.

Dumarest said, "What does she do? Stare into a crystal ball?"

"Don't scoff, darling. She's clever. You'll see."

She pressed on, through the rollers of an air-lock, down a gallery, into the outer section dominated by booths and sideshows. The place was empty now; the circus had yet to come to life. Beyond a flap painted with garish symbols a candle flickered in a crested bowl. In its light the cowled figure sitting hunched in a chair behind a table looked shrunken and dead.

"Krystyna?" Reiza stepped closer to the table. "Are you asleep? I know it's a bad time but—"

"Step aside, child. I know why you are here."

An elementary trick of the trade; why else should people come to a fortune teller but to have their fortunes told? One augmented by others; the candle with its flickering, disguising flame, the tang of incense with its misting fumes, arcane symbols and mysterious objects. The woman herself.

She was old, gnarled with passing years, her face seamed and scored deep with a mesh of lines. The cowl framed it with kindly shadows and provided a setting for her eyes. Small, deep-set, palely blue and as penetrating as a tempered blade.

"Sit!" The hand matched the face, twisted, a blunted claw marred with lumps. Her voice was the thin rustle of dried leaves in a winter's gale. "Sit!" Again the hand stabbed at the chair facing her across the table. "You hesitate, young man. Do you doubt my powers?"

"No, Mother." Dumarest sat in the proffered chair. "I know you are expert at what you do."

"A sly tongue. Do you mock me?"

"No." Dumarest was genuine in his denial. "I would never do that."

A woman, old, twisted with crippling infirmities, fighting the hampering effect of her afflictions. One alone or with a youngster to whom she would teach her trade. Paying her way and giving her clients what they expected. For that, if nothing else, she deserved respect.

"There is truth in you," she said. "And kindness. And, I think, some mercy."

"And love," said Reiza. "That too."

"Love," said the old woman. "Always they want to be loved. To find love and be given it. Well, I tell them what they want to hear and more often than not things they would be better not knowing. A fault, but I grow old and impatient. Why peer into the future if you are afraid of what you might see? Death, despair, pain, betrayal—such things are inevitable. But I try to be kind. Always I try to be that.''

Conning the punters with slick words and facile phrases. Quizzing them by indirection, milking them of details to be fed back later in different words and subtle suggestions. Using misdirection, hesitation, ambiguity and guile to weave the client into a mesh of self-betrayal. An art at which Dumarest guessed she was an expert.

"You know too much," she said. "And, at the same time, not enough. For those I choose I give genuine service. But, you understand, I cannot be precise as to moments of time. Nor as to exact means of action. Events take their own time and operate in their own manner. For example, that you will die is inevitable. But just how and when—''

"You warned of Hayter's death," said Reiza. "You said how he would end.''

"A man plays with fire—what are the chances of his getting burned?" A shrug moved the fabric of the cowled robe. "Some things are obvious and cast their shadow before them. Others—'' Again the shrug. "Give me your palm.''

Dumarest felt the twisted fingers grasp his own as he obeyed. A nail traced a path, paused, traced another.

"No." She released his hand. "For you there is a better way. Here!''

Dumarest looked at the stack of cards she set before him. Old, the backs a mass of complex lines, cracked but bearing the gleam of applied polish. The size was wrong for a normal deck.

"Shuffle them," said Krystyna. "Run them through your hands. Impregnate them with your personal magnetism. Their order will illustrate your fate.''

"Do it," urged Reiza. "Please, Earl.''

Dumarest picked up the cards, riffled them, shuffled with a gambler's skill.

The old woman said, "You handle them well. You know what they are?''

"Yes.''

"Then cut them into two piles. Rest a hand on each and concentrate on your present situation. Then shuffle again and hand them to me.''

She waited until it was done then sat with the deck poised in her hands.

"Once, so legend has it, these were the only cards known. Men depicted gods and natural hazards thinking that the symbol gave dominance over the thing and that, by controlling a part of the universe, they could govern the whole. They were wrong but later, perhaps because men grew afraid of alien places and needed something to guide them, the original pack was enlarged to what it is today. Every hazard and circumstance which could affect a person was isolated, compacted and illustrated to form the Arcana Universalis. Fire, flood, storm, war, space, bursting suns. Of course each symbol has extended meanings. For example space does not just mean the void between the stars but a gap, a distance, a setting apart. The art lies in the interpretation. I could set out these cards and you would see things of personal import but because you have intimate knowledge of your life your vision would be narrowed against the wider implications. And you, child—" She glanced at Reiza. "You know even less and so would look for what you wanted to see. Love, fecundity, happiness. I?" The eyes closed, opened again. "I read the truth."

Her twisted fingers slid a card from the top of the deck and laid it face-down on the table before Dumarest.

"Your card," she told him. "Your significator."

She spread others around in a ritual pattern, face-up, bright symbols glowing in the guttering light of the candle. Reiza drew in her breath as the skeleton appeared.

"Earl—"

"Death," said Krystyna. "The fate which waits us all. But also it is a transformation. Here it signifies an end; the cards before it carry your fate."

She gloomed over them, a finger touching, passing on, her withered lips pursing, moving as if she mumbled esoteric incantations. Dumarest watched with inward amusement. Beside him Reiza was a coiled spring.

"Earl," she whispered. "I'm frightened. I shouldn't have brought you here. If the reading is bad—God! How can I bear to lose you?"

He said, "There's nothing to be afraid of. It's just a game."

"A game?" Krystyna lifted her head with a sudden motion and sat poised like a snake about to strike. "Aye," she said after a moment. "A game as all life is a game. One I can read—or would you prefer not to know the things which wait?"

"Let's go, Earl." Reiza tugged at his arm. "It was a mistake to come. Please, Earl."

"No." He freed his arm, his eyes holding those of the old woman. "When you're ready, Mother."

Again she brooded over the cards.

"First the beginning for the child is father to the man and as the twig is bent so the tree will grow." Her finger touched a card next to the significator. "The Egg, symbol of life and fertility but also of change for from the egg springs a different form. And this is touched by conflict, desolation, catastrophe." The finger moved from card to card, pausing at the depiction of a man dressed in tattered garments, smiling, a staff bearing a bundle resting on one shoulder. "The Rover. Restless, always moving, ever seeking the unknown beyond the horizon. A fool, some would say, leaving reality in pursuit of a dream. A man without faith and faith is not for him." The finger moved to the symbol of a priest, the card reversed. "The comfort of spiritual assurance is absent and he lacks the support of the church. But it does not work against him for it lies on the dexter side. A neutrality. This is not." The finger moved, came to rest. "The Cradle. Also reversed and therefore empty. There will be no fruitful issues or successful outcomes."

"No." Reiza dug her fingers into Dumarest's arm as she whispered the denial. "She's wrong, Earl. She has to be."

He rested his hand on hers, giving her the comfort of his touch as the old woman droned on. Looking at the cards she touched, the Wheel, the Ship, the Pylon. Reiza drew in her breath as the gnarled finger came to rest on the Skull.

"Deceit," said Krystyna. "Poison of the mind and even of the body. Threats of a secret nature. Associated with knowledge." Her finger tapped the Book, moved to a card meshed with a web and an eight-legged creature. "The Spider. Already you are deep in the snare of its spinning and the danger of the skull warns of its intention. But the Book?"

She fell silent, brooding over the cards, checking their association. Reiza was too impatient to wait.

"Tell us," she blurted. "Krystyna—what do you see?"

"Death." The old woman leaned back, her eyes winking points of brilliance in the guttering light as she looked at Dumarest. "You are enmeshed in danger and deception which can have only one end. How it will come and from what source has yet to be revealed." Her hand reached for the face-down card which represented Dumarest then, abruptly, she drew it back. "No. You do it. A man should find his own destiny."

Dumarest reached out, took the card, turned it. In the dim lighting the figure it depicted seemed made of blood. Tall, thin, the scarlet robe it wore emblazoned with the Cyclan Seal.

"Logic." Krystyna added, "The fifteenth card. Fifteen—the number of your fate."

CHAPTER SEVEN

Master Marle, Cyber Prime, woke to stare into darkness broken only by a single point of light which relieved the stygian gloom of the chamber. A matter of efficiency; total darkness would prove hampering in case of emergency; time wasted as eyes grew accustomed to the light, movement disorganized. Now he lay supine as his body geared itself to a higher degree of function. Minutes which grew longer as the years progressed for no matter how efficient the basic mechanism the aging process took its toll.

"Master." The voice followed a bell. "Time to wake, Master."

A summons repeated, dying as his finger touched a control. Another and the light strengthened to reveal the bleak outlines of the room. One devoid of all but functional units, lacking decoration, cell-like in its Spartan simplicity.

Marle rose, swinging his legs over the edge of the bed, sitting and waiting as his body accepted the higher demand. The clock showed it to be night on the surface but here, in the caverns sunken deep, the divisions of light and darkness held no meaning. Time was governed by the segments of hours. He had slept four of them, waking minutes before the alarm. Once, not long ago now, he would have woken seconds before the bell.

A thought he took with him as he showered, feeling no pleasure from the lash of water against his flesh. To bathe was a matter of hygiene, a necessity as were other functional demands. As was the food he ate when, cleansed and dressed, he sat to a frugal meal.

85

Prolo bowed as he entered his office. "Master, I have placed—"

"A moment." The aide was new, replacing Wyeth who had gone to his reward. A good man and a dedicated servant of the Cyclan, but as yet a little unaccustomed to his new position. "Any news from the laboratories?"

"As regards the affinity twin? None, Master, all negative as before."

"Matters of prime importance should always be given precedence," said Marle. "And to repeat the obvious is to be inefficient. Any news of Avro?"

"None." The rebuke had stung even though deserved yet the aide's face remained passive. "His condition is as before."

A statement of the obvious and another demonstration of inefficiency—if there was no news the condition could not have changed and so to have mentioned it was a waste of both words and time. Prolo would learn, and soon, or the aide would be replaced. And, if he was, an investigation would be held to discover why a man so flawed had been allowed to rise so high.

Marle glanced at his desk where reports rested in a neat pile. Prolo had stacked them and if his judgment was at fault it was the last mistake he would make.

Alone Marle studied them. The first required his immediate decision and he gave it into a recorder.

"Report XDB 13572. Prince Tyner must be deposed. Arrange his death before the Omphale Festival. Throw blame on the Kaspar faction. Cease all imports of penka from Nemcova."

A classic situation; Prince Tyner, young, idealistic, wanted to free his people from their dependence on expensive imports. Dead, his friends accused, trade threatened by the lack of penka, confusion would be accelerated by the festival. From the chaos an older ruler would rise to seize power. One aided and advised by the Cyclan.

The next report was of lesser urgency and Marle gave thought to the most efficient way of resolving the problem. A matter of trade dependency which could yield to the impetus of a new discovery.

The number then, "Instruct the resident cyber on Chroneld to release the formulae for the synthesization of ondret to the Smyslov Laboratories."

Within two years the farms of Chroneld would be ruined as the artificial product rendered their crops superfluous. Desperation would induce civil war and to retain their power the rulers would need help. The Cyclan would give it—at a price. And one more world would fall to the domination of logic and reason.

Quickly Marle ran through the rest of the reports. Prolo had done his job and earned a remand. His previous errors could have been the result of too great a desire to appear efficient, but with time he would learn. Learn and take his place at the side of the most powerful man the galaxy had ever known.

Marle recognized the error and corrected it. Not the man but the organization which he served. The Cyclan which dominated a host of planets, working always from positions behind established authority. Ruling cadres and princes who, desperate to maintain their hold, had turned to the Cyclan for advice.

The service had been given for a fee, but the initial payment was merely the beginning. Once the client had tasted the power at their disposal they wanted more, more. For a cyber, any cyber, could take a handful of facts and from them extrapolate the most probable sequence of events. Not true prophecy but calculated assessment of available data and a prediction of what most likely would happen. Predictions so accurate that they seemed like actual announcements of what was to come. With such information a ruler could maintain his power, a trader grow rich, a mercenary always win or, if not win, never lose.

Then, once their need was recognized and relied on, the Cyclan moved to formulate its own purpose.

Marle rose and touched a control, the chamber darkening as, within it, a simulacrum of the galaxy flared to life. A host of minute points, blurs, streamers of luminous gas. At such a small scale details were lost; individual planets, rogue moons, wandering asteroids. But the stars remained and a wide scatter of them were marked in red.

The scarlet of the Cyclan—the color marking their conquests.

Soon the scarlet would have spread to engulf entire areas of space. Eventually it would dominate all and then there would be an end of waste, of futile effort, of wasted resources. Logic and reason would replace the idiocy of emotional response. The old, sick, crippled and nonproductive would be eliminated. The inefficient. The maladjusted. The human race would become a smoothly functioning machine, each ability and mind directed to the solving of all the problems of the universe.

And he, now, was at the head of the Cyclan.

Power such as no one had ever hoped to attain before. At his decision men died, worlds were ravaged, others urged into the fruitfulness which was their potential. But all flecked with the scarlet touch, even though unknowingly, obeyed, without question, himself as their ruler.

A power which would last as long as he proved himself capable of using it.

"Master?" Prolo calling on the intercom. "Master?"

His face appeared as Marle touched a control.

"What is it?"

"Avro, Master. There has been a positive response."

Tyzach met him as Marle entered the laboratory. The place held a variety of instruments, a bed surrounded by monitors, assistants who stood at a respectful distance. They, like the physician, wore laboratory clothing. Only Marle warmed the chamber with his scarlet robe.

"Master." Tyzach's nod was acknowledgment of superior rank. "There has been no improvement."

"But you did obtain a positive response?"

"Ten minutes ago."

It had been minor and inconclusive but the first obtained since Avro had been brought back to Cyclan Headquarters from the world named Heaven.

Marle moved to where he lay on the bed. He was naked, wires wreathing his emaciated body, his shaven skull. A corpselike creature, old, withered, the skin taut over prominent bone. Stripped, Marle would have looked his twin.

But Avro had failed while he had not.

To Tyzach he said, "We know that Dumarest injected him with the dominant half of the affinity twin. The host was a local life-form. Is it possible, now that there is evidence the bond is weakening, for you to isolate the portion of the affinity twin within his brain?"

"No." Tyzach was positive. "In theory it should be possible but the affinity twin nestles deep in the cortex and, as far as we can determine, changes its nature once activated by the host. A deeper examination than we have as yet made would lead to inevitable death."

A small loss; Avro's failure had merited his extinction. Not for him the reward Wyeth had obtained, his body reduced to ash, his living, thinking brain now sealed in a capsule and a part of

Central Intelligence. The reward all cybers enjoyed unless they proved themselves inefficient.

Yet to dig into the brain would be to kill all hope of potential knowledge.

A dilemma resolved as soon as recognized. Avro would live, yield whatever knowledge he possessed and then, if the action was promising of added knowledge, would be dissected.

Nothing must stand in the way of obtaining the secret of the affinity twin.

The secret stolen from the Cyclan and passed on to Dumarest.

Marle turned and paced the laboratory, thinking of those who had failed and what had happened to them. A punishment directed as example, not revenge. To regret the past was a waste of time. Such emotion was alien to any cyber as were love and fear and hate and physical pleasure. An operation performed on the thalamus when young together with rigorous training had freed them of the poison afflicting the human race. Replacing it with reason and cold logic. Tools with which to reshape the universe.

But which, as yet, had failed to capture the one man who held the secret. The sequence in which the fifteen biomolecular units forming the affinity twin had to be joined.

"Master." Tyzach was beside the bed checking the monitors. "Another response."

"To applied stimuli?"

"Yes. I'm shortening the period."

Stabbing the brain and body with demanding current. Shocking the system into a reaction other than that of the autonomous process which had kept the heart beating, the lungs breathing, the body moving in a self-preserving pattern. Raised to his feet Avro would stand, would move if pushed without falling. Would void his system of waste and ingest food and water. A mindless vegetable of less worth than an insect.

At such times it was hard to remember that the sharp intelligence Avro possessed was not dead but merely absent. Lodged in another brain belonging to a creature far distant on another world.

"Quickly." Tyzach called to an assistant. "Raise stimulating power one degree."

A stronger thrust of energy rewarded by the kick of a needle, the movement of pens tracing lines on a rolling sheet of paper. An encephalogram, another record to add to the rest. In the search for the affinity twin no scrap of data could be overlooked or ignored.

"Again." Marle broke the silence as the body on the bed remained inert. "There should be some muscular reaction by now. Increase the stimulus."

"That would not be wise." Tyzach was firm in his objection. "For the bond to be broken the host-body must die. If the released intelligence has nowhere to return then it will dissipate. A stronger stimulus, applied now, might destroy those few cells within the cortex which could be of paramount importance."

A guess but a good one and, failing all concrete evidence to the contrary, might well be true. If Marle insisted his suggestion be followed, and the result should be less than successful, his own efficiency would be thrown into doubt.

He stepped back, arms folded, hands thrust into the wide sleeves of his robe. A gaunt and watchful pillar of flame. One who noted every detail as his mind expanded to engulf a vast section of the cosmos. The world on which Avro's intelligence was lodged—how did he see it? How did he assess it? How easily did he manipulate the host body? How efficient was the transfer?

The early studies had been staggering in their implications, the data promising incredible powers. The affinity twin could give the old a new, a young and virile body. A bribe no man or woman could resist. But it went much further than that. The mind of a cyber could be placed within the brain and body of a ruler. Gone would be the need for tedious manipulation of events. Decisions, once made, could be acted on without delay.

The Cyclan could rule the entire galaxy within a matter of decades.

A dream of power soon to be regained and Marle felt the euphoria of it. The glow of mental achievement which was the only pleasure he could know.

"A positive increase in neurological activity." One of the assistants reported to Tyzach. "Synaptic time-lag decreasing."

"Muscular response?"

"Improving."

"Apply vibro-massage to extremities." Tyzach added, "Note muscular contraction rate and build up of fatigue toxins."

Marle said, "The encephalograph?"

"Functioning on both prime and secondary levels of cortical activity. Scintillometers are tracing neutron paths within the cortex."

"Electronic scan of the basic area?"

"No, for the reason already given. The dominant half of the affinity twin must not be influenced. Once the subject has woken a full scan can be made."

"Heart-beat accelerating." The voice of the assistant maintained the even modulation devoid of any irritant factors, the vocal hallmark of all cybers. A moment then, "Master! He wakes."

Avro opened his eyes.

The bowl held a nourishing soup scientifically composed so as to give the maximum of energy-potential together with essential minerals. With it had come a portion of bread with a high percentage of roughage. Fuel for the engine which was his body, but even as he ate it Avro remembered other foods, unfamiliar tastes.

A time in which he had been an angel.

He leaned back, closing his eyes, recalling the rush and pressure of air, the strain of outspread wings as he had ridden the uprising thermals. A thing which had happened in a flash, his mind leaving his body as it fell from the prick of a needle. For a long moment he had been disorganized, the host body failing, wheeling as it fell to the rocks below, then its autonomous system came to the rescue and the pinions carried it up and safely away.

Flying.

Flying as no man had ever flown before.

Now it was over and he was back in his own body among his own kind. They had fed him, bathed him, checked his body and mind, questioned him with probing efficiency. Now, fed again, he was to learn his fate.

Marle looked up from his desk as Avro entered the office remaining silent until the aide had left them alone.

Without preamble he said, "It is the decision of the Council that you failed in your mission. Do you agree with their finding?"

"No."

"You claim to have succeeded?"

"Not wholly." Avro continued, "There are degrees of success. I went to find Dumarest and I found him. That was not failure."

"You went to capture him," corrected Marle. "You elected to do so and the Council met your every demand as regards supplies and men. A special ship. A special crew. The entire resources of the Cyclan placed at your disposal. Yet you returned with nothing. Dumarest eluded you and retains the secret of the affinity twin. We still lack the correct sequence in which the fifteen units must be assembled. The Council has determined that your lack of positive results illustrates your inefficiency and merits the penalty of failure.''

Total extinction, both body and brain reduced to ash. His personal awareness, his ego, destroyed along with the rest.

Avro felt an inward chill as he considered it. An unusual reaction; as a cyber he should be a stranger to fear. And the punishment was normal; the penalty paid by all who failed. Marle himself would suffer the same end should he demonstrate his inefficiency.

Avro said, ''I failed to effect Dumarest's capture, that is true, but even in defeat things can be learned.''

''Not to underestimate your opponent?''

''I did not underestimate him. But his luck, the factor which seems to play such a prominent part in his like and which I suspect stems from some paraphysical source, saved him yet again. But I am not wholly to blame. The crew failed to operate with the expected efficiency. No matter what happened to me they should have taken Dumarest.''

A mistake—explained by the debilitating effects of the journey, bluff, fear of losing their quarry, of killing their superior.

Dumarest was clever, Marle had never doubted it, but only now had he come to appreciate how elusive the man had made himself. Was it because of some paraphysical power he possessed? Certainly his luck seemed incredible at times. A trap set, sprung— and still he had managed to escape. Using the dedication of the servants of the Cyclan to their master to aid his plan.

What had it been like to fly?

Avro had done his best to tell them; spools of tape were filled with his report, but none of them could convey what he must have really known. Dead that knowledge would be lost. Alive it could be used to spur him to greater efforts.

Avro said, as if following the other's thoughts, ''I know Dumarest now better than before. I've met him face to face, talked with him, tested his resolution. Incorporated into previous data the experience could be the turning point. The next time I shall not fail.''

''Are you asking for another chance?''

''Eliminating me will gain the Cyclan nothing. If I try and

again fail what would have been lost? To discard a useful tool is both illogical and inefficient.''

Arguments bolstering Marle's own conviction. Avro had lived too long, had served too well not to have value. His failure must be punished but total extinction need not be the answer. Not now. Not when he could be of use.

The depiction of the galaxy blossomed into life as Marle touched a control. It expanded as he operated another, stars streaming outward from the center to cast swaths and streaks of transient brilliance over their faces and robes, the utilitarian furnishings of the office. As it settled he indicated a glowing point, a tiny speck beside it.

"There," he said. "Heaven."

A world of soft winds and soaring hills, of rolling plains and wide-stretching seas. Of crystalline nests hugging precipitous faces. Of winged figures which rose to wheel and dive and rise again.

And, suddenly, Avro was an angel again.

He felt the lash of wind against his face and body, relived the euphoria induced by the thrumming pulse of blood through veins and arteries, the drumbeat of his heart loud in his ears. Rising to soar, to glide while beneath him the terrain shrank to the dimensions of a toy. To lunge at others of his own kind, to drive off arrogant males, to circle the females, ushering them back to the nest.

"Avro." Marle was facing him, his eyes questing. "Is something wrong?"

"No." Avro drew air deep into his lungs. "It is nothing."

"The report on your physical condition stated that you are close to optimum function. There has been some loss of tissue, but that was to be expected despite the intravenous feeding during your journey back and the period here before your intelligence returned. And yet then, for a moment, you seemed about to collapse."

"A slight nausea." Avro corrected the statement, to be sick was to prove the inadequacy of the body. "A lack of immediate coordination of mind and eye." He gestured at the depiction. "The retinal musculature has been at rest too long. Exercise will correct it."

Marle nodded, dismissing the subject, Avro was the best judge of his condition. Again he faced the depiction and the planet he'd indicated.

"Heaven," he said again. "A world of little value even though the dominant avian life form holds a certain interest. From it Dumarest travelled to Aumont."

"When?"

"Shortly after you were stricken. The captain of your vessel did his best to make the most of the situation in which he found himself. He could not attack for fear of destroying Dumarest and he had also to safeguard your person. Leaving the world, he headed far out into space and there hung in a position to monitor the other ship. A chance which succeeded; his instruments were of a superior quality. He could register the other vessel but the reverse did not apply. He waited long enough to track their direction of flight."

"They could have altered course."

"A possibility but of no importance. Dumarest landed on Aumont. Word had been sent ahead to our cybers and agents in the area and he was spotted. He left before action could be taken, first to Kreuz then to Tolen and then to Ceruti. There the ship was seized by our agents."

"And Dumarest?"

"Missing. He had left the ship either on Kreuz or Tolen. Both are busy worlds with many vessels offering a choice of routes and directions." Marle's tone did not change as he added, "Which ship would he have taken? To which world would he have gone?"

A test; Marle would already have made the prediction and was now examining his ability. On the outcome could hang his fate. Avro studied the data which flashed on a wall; details of ships, cargoes, destinations, times. Dumarest would have been aware of his danger; a man on the run doing his best to delude his pursuers. Shifting in a random pattern and avoiding the obvious. But no pattern could be wholly random; each choice had to be dictated by the man himself and each would be governed by personal and subconscious idiosyncrasies. A dislike of the color red—and a ship so painted would be avoided. A dislike of cold, of mountains, of roaring winds. A reluctance to share a cabin. A fondness for warm climes. A host of minor spurs unsuspected by the quarry but glaring signposts to the hunters.

And Avro had studied every aspect of Dumarest's behavior known to the Cyclan.

"Schike," he said. "Dumarest would have traveled on the *Hoyland* to Schike."

"And then?"

"The *Vladek* to Caltoon." A small world on the edge of a busy cluster, one on which no cyber would find a use for his services but where a man could lose himself in a crowd. "And then to Ostrogoth."

And from there?

Avro checked the data. A normal man, even though aware of pursuit, would follow a predictable path, but Dumarest was far from ordinary. A man to take the obvious because it was just that, to bluff and counter-bluff, to do the unsuspected. Like traveling to Vanch with its continual rain. Or Leasdale with its icy seas. Bad worlds both and Dumarest would not want to be stranded. Where then?

Where?

"Baatz." Marle supplied the answer. Avro had demonstrated his ability, to continue the test would be inefficient. "Dumarest is on Baatz at the circus of Chen Wei. Cyber Tron is on his way to ensure his capture or to take possession of him should the capture have been made."

"And if he should escape?"

"He will not."

"The possibility exists," said Avro. "Nothing can be one hundred percent certain. Always there is the unknown factor. Tron is a stranger to Dumarest, he has yet to learn of his wiles. He could be overconfident. It has happened before."

Too often and with too many dead cybers to add to the failures. A fact Marle knew as he was aware that, should Dumarest escape again, the blame would be his.

He said, "I place you in charge of Dumarest's capture and return. You will leave immediately." He added, in a tone bleak despite its even modulation, "You failed once, Avro—do not fail again."

CHAPTER EIGHT

Valaban said, "Settle down, Earl. The way you pace about is making me nervous. Quit it before you disturb the beasts."

Good advice and Dumarest took it, taking his place beside the old man on a bench. Around him stretched the cavernous area beneath the stands, one split and sectioned to avoid waste, the part reserved for the animals thick with smells.

He drew them into his nostrils, recognizing the tang of sweat, dung, oils, embrocation, urine. An odor too similar to another he knew but this, at least, was free of the reek of blood.

"You're restless," said Valaban. "I can sense it and so can the animals. Here." He held out a bottle. "Take a drink of this—it will calm you."

"Thanks." Dumarest took the bottle, held it to his lips, threw back his head and pretended to drink. Handing it back he said, "So you never met Chen Wei. Who owned the circus before Shakira?"

"Damned if I know." Valaban frowned at the single lamp which illuminated the area. A pool of light in a darkness edged with cages and gleaming, watchful eyes. "It was a long time ago now. Maybe Chen Wei did, I only said I'd never met him. Burski hired me. He got himself killed on Daleth—a fight over a woman as I remember, then Shakira took over. That must be, oh, close to thirty years ago."

A long time in a transient society and if Valaban lacked the answers they weren't to be found.

He stiffened as noise came from a cage, relaxing as it died.

97

"The klachen," he grunted. "The damned thing's more trouble than it's worth. Zucco must have been crazy to take it on."

"Maybe he likes its rider?" A lithe young girl with a rounded face and slanted, enigmatic eyes, she danced on the platform of the creature's back with stunning agility. "Is he like that?"

"What man isn't if he gets the chance?" Valaban shrugged. "But Kiki's too tame for him, too docile. He likes strength in a woman, something he can beat down, use, conquer. I guess you know what he is."

"I know."

"Then you know enough to be careful. Stay away from him. Maybe he'll forget you're around."

A warning? Dumarest looked at Valaban, studying the seamed face, the sunken eyes. An old man with an inner wisdom who would see more than he admitted and know more than he was willing to tell. But some information had been gained; small details which added to build a picture. Zucco, for example, a man who had joined the circus some five years earlier and who seemed to possess no special skills. One who had climbed fast and high. Dumarest wondered why.

"You're good, Earl," said Valaban. "I appreciate you helping me out. You've a way with animals. Some have it and some don't and no one knows just what it is. Trust, maybe, or just an absence of fear. You don't scare them." He frowned as, again, the klachen kicked at the bars of its cage.

Dumarest said, "When the circus moves do the beasts go with it?"

"Not all. We sell them off for breeding stock mostly, that's why none of the males has been neutered. Most can easily be trained but some can't. The cats, for instance, they come from Flyte. Special mutated stock bred for guardians. You know Flyte?"

"No."

"It's a prison world. Jungle and cleared areas ringed with wire. Outside the cats are allowed to roam free. Sometimes a prisoner tries to escape and when he does the authorities write him off. The cats get him," Valaban explained. "Use him for sport. If he's lucky he dies fast."

"Has Reiza had them long?"

"Since they were kittens. Shakira bought them for her. I cut their claws and blunted their fangs and she used to sleep with them. To build an affinity, you understand. Before they will

98

obey they must accept her as one of themselves." Valaban paused then added, "Maybe she became more like them than she realized. A creature of whims and fancies and sudden impulses. Hayter said that once." He glanced at Dumarest. "You know about Hayter?"

"Her dead lover? Yes, I know. The cats killed him, didn't they?"

Valaban took a sip from his bottle and lowered it to stare at the lamp.

"Hayter was a good man and I liked him. The cats ripped out his life but I figure he was dead before he entered the ring. His mind wasn't on the job which was bad enough but I think there was something more. An animal," he said. "But walking on two legs like a man."

Zucco? A possibility, he had become Reiza's lover and Hayter's death had been a convenient accident. If it had been an accident.

Dumarest said, casually, "I've heard of such things. Used them at times when hunting for a living. A special mix which attracts the prey. A scent they can't resist and I suppose you could make one which would induce an attack. Was it something like that?"

"Maybe."

"You didn't spot it?"

"Hayter was covered in blood and his stomach was a mess. The stink was enough to cover all others but I remember, just before he went into the ring, he dabbed at his face with a cloth. To dry the sweat, I guess, but he could have been putting something on as well as taking it off."

"Did you tell any of this to Shakira?"

"I tried but he didn't seem to want to listen. And who am I to go up against his man? Not that I give a damn for any of them. With my skills I can go anywhere. Every farmer will want a man who can handle his beasts and this isn't the only circus in the galaxy." Valaban used his bottle again. "Maybe it's time to quit the way it's being run."

"Zucco?"

"It's not just him. Every circus needs a strong ringmaster but there are other things."

"Like too many empty seats?"

"You've noticed," said Valaban. "The take's too low. We've been here too long and lost our novelty. We should be up and moving to greener fields. In the old days this place would be on

99

its way by now. The animals sold, acts thinned, half the tents deflated and packed. We even started—'' He broke off, rearing to his feet as the klachen screamed its rage. ''What the hell's going on?''

Metal clanged and, suddenly, the creature was before them.

It was the size of a horse, scaled, the head like that of a lizard. A vestigial tail ended in a knotted mass of bone and spine, the feet tipped with round and blunted claws. Beneath the hide and across the broad platform of its back muscle rippled in smoothly coordinated motion.

''Freeze!'' Valaban's voice, while gentle, held the snap of command. ''Something's scared it. Move and you'll make it worse. Leave this to me.'' He faced the animal, talking as he moved slowly toward the creature. ''Easy, now. Easy. Just rest easy, now. Easy.''

Words which became a soothing drone directed at the lifted head, the orifices of the ears. A demonstration of his skill, the talent which gave him mastery over the majority of animals. Dumarest remembered a man he'd once known who could calm the most frenzied horse by whispering in its ear. Valaban had the same attribute but the klachen wasn't a horse and, if it charged, the old man would be dead.

And Dumarest knew it would charge.

Knew it with the instinct which had served him so often before. Even as Valaban stepped closer Dumarest was on the move. A lunge which closed the space between them, sent his shoulder slamming into the other man, hurling him down and to one side.

Falling beside him as the beast tore past where he had stood.

''Earl! I—''

''Your bottle!'' Dumarest climbed to his feet. He didn't look at the other man. ''Give me your bottle!''

His knife was in his hand ready to slash and stab but used it would fill the air with the scent of fresh blood. An odor which would madden the other beasts within the area into a destructive outburst. Already they deafened him with their snarls and growls, the metallic clash as they fought the confines of their cages.

''Leave this to me, Earl.'' Valaban, shaken, was on his feet beside Dumarest. ''I know how to handle it.''

''Get close and it will kill you.'' Dumarest pointed to where the klachen stood, head weaving, nostrils dilated as it snuffed the air. "You can't move fast enough to dodge. Now give me that bottle and your blouse. Or something to hold the liquid. Move!"

Time was against them. The creature, disturbed, could run amok. But to wait was to allow its fear to build, to explode in a killing fury.

"Here!" Valaban handed over the bottle and a blanket. He watched as Dumarest tore loose the cork and spilled the fluid over the material. "You going to blind it?"

"I'm going to try." Dumarest sheathed his knife. "Stand ready. Once I get this over its head it'll start to rear. When it calms run forward and do your stuff."

He edged forward before Valaban could answer, the blanket in his hands, booted feet silent on the floor. As the scaled head turned toward him he froze, standing motionless until the ruby eyes had moved away. Closer, he froze again, the blanket held high before him, the smell of the fluid masking his scent. As the head turned away he was running, jumping high to land on the broad back, the blanket falling to wrap around the head, blinding the eyes.

As it settled the klachen exploded into violent action.

Dumarest felt the surge and lift of muscle, the jarring impact as the creature landed. He slipped, almost fell as the beast reared, clamped his legs tight as it darted forward and came to a sudden halt. A moment in which he tasted blood and felt the strain on nerve and sinew then the animal was rearing again, the tail lashing to free itself of the rider on its back.

"Earl! Watch it!"

Dumarest heard Valaban's yell of warning and felt the blow which scraped over his spine. One which would have knocked him to the ground with a shattered back if he hadn't heaved himself forward to lock his thighs around the base of the klachen's neck. A hold he maintained as the creature threshed beneath him, stooping forward to wrap the blanket over the jaws, twisting to clamp them shut. Locking the fabric with his left hand he pressed his right over the nostrils, blocking the passage of air and filling the beast's lungs with the fumes of Valaban's bottle.

Choked, near to asphyxiation, the creature slowed its wild lungings, came at last to a quivering rest.

"You've got it," said Valaban. "You can leave the rest to me." He came close, moving the blanket as Dumarest released his grip, his voice low as he stroked the scaled head.

Dumarest watched, waiting, then as the old man looked up

and nodded he slid from his position to land softly at the side of the klachen. As Valaban continued to soothe the beast he stepped over to its cage.

The lock was simple but far too sophisticated to ever be released by an animal. Dumarest checked the cage and the area around it. The rear was masked in shadows which blurred detail and he stood among them looking toward the bench and the single lamp. Someone with a stick could easily have opened the cage without being seen. He moved farther back to where a wall rested close to the bars. The smooth surface gaped in a long, vertical cut. Dumarest fingered the material; thin plastic meant only for a flimsy screen. At the base of the cut a silken scarf rested like a smear of yellow.

One bearing a perfume he recognized.

"Reiza's." Valaban snuffed at the fabric. "That's her perfume."

"You certain?"

"She wears it like a brand. It's hers all right." Valaban glowered at the scarf. "Expensive stuff. Zucco bought her a bottle once and she's worn nothing else since. But why would she want to open the cage?"

Dumarest said, dryly, "One reason might be to kill you."

"Not Reiza. Why should she want that?"

"Someone opened the cage," said Dumarest. "That same person must have tormented the klachen. Whoever it was knew that you'd come running when it screamed."

"And if it hadn't been for you I'd be dead by now." Valaban drew in his breath, the scarf ripping between his hands. "Cats," he said bitterly. "You can make a fuss of them, spoil them, talk to them and make them purr. They'll let you stroke them and scratch their ears and roll over all as friendly and nice as you could want. Then, as you turn, they'll rip out your spine." The shredded scarf fell to lie at his feet. "Cats and women—you can't trust either."

In the crowd a girl was crying; big tears running over rounded cheeks, a fuzzy-haired doll clutched to the faded dress she wore. She seemed lost and afraid and looking at the adult world with brimming blue eyes.

"Hello, there!" Dumarest knelt before her. "Can't find your way?"

"I turned," she sobbed. "And when I looked back they were gone."

"Your mother and father?"

"And Ingred and Uncle Mac. I've looked and looked but they've vanished. They've left me!" The tears ran faster over her cheeks. "I'm all alone!"

A small tragedy and one easily resolved but, to the child, a frightening experience.

"We'll find them," promised Dumarest. "Would you like to ride on my shoulder? Could you hang on?" He straightened as she nodded. "Right then. Ready? Up we go!"

A lift and she was perched high, the doll firm beneath one arm, the other locked around his neck. A clown called to her and waved, another whistled; novelties which dried her tears as Dumarest walked down the gallery toward the information desk. The woman on duty smiled.

"Another lost one? Well, set her down." She waved to where a cushioned area held a few stuffed animals, a ball, some scattered toys. "What's your name, dear? Celi? That's a nice name." She looked at Dumarest. "I can take care of this now. Thanks for bringing her."

He nodded and walked on. The crowd was thin for the time of day; late afternoon was prime for those on vacation or with a day off from work. Later would be better but if it was like the pattern of others, it would be far from what was desired. Poor attendances led to bad performances from those operating the sideshows. Already most would be grumbling.

Krystyna would be one of them.

Only a couple of clients waited outside her booth instead of the normal dozen and they were a pair wanting a joint reading. They dived through the flap as a woman emerged to stand, looking vaguely about, blinking as she saw Dumarest.

"Tall," she murmured. "All in gray—how did she know?"

A glimpse caught from a mirror reflecting the external scene and Dumarest could guess what the woman had been told. A stranger, waiting, who could guide her on her way. One who would steer her decision.

She said, "Pardon me, but could you—I mean, would you help me? She," a hand lifted to gesture toward the booth, "She said you would."

"How can I help?"

"Give me a color. Black or blond. Quickly now."

"Black." She was a brunette, young, and it was easy to guess torn with indecision over an emotional affair. Two suitors—which should she choose? The old woman had craftily avoided any chance of being placed in the wrong.

"Black—that's Marek. I'm glad. So glad!" Her smile was radiant. "Thank you. Thank you so much!"

For telling her what she had wanted to hear. Dumarest watched her move away then thrust himself into the booth as the couple left. It was as he remembered; a shadowed dimness lit by a single, guttering flame. In her chair the cowled figure waited, silent as he slipped into the chair.

"Give me your hand."

He extended it, frowning, the voice though dry was not as he remembered. He caught the hand which moved toward his palm, gripped it, held it as he threw back the shielding cowl.

"Where's Krystyna?"

"Please!" The girl was young, her face marred by furrows which had torn her cheek and ruined her nose and upper lip. "The cowl."

Dumarest watched as the face disappeared into kindly darkness. An apprentice or someone filling in. The former, he guessed, for someone so scarred and lacking the funds to have the damage repaired opportunities of earning a living would be few.

She said, "If you want a reading give me your hand."

"No, give me yours." He heard the sudden intake of her breath as he ran a coin over her palm. "You've been badly taught, girl. Always have your hand crossed with silver before doing anything else. Here." He dropped the coin into her palm. "Where's Krystyna?"

"Resting."

"At this time of day?" He guessed the reason. "Is she just tired—or sick?"

He knew the answer as soon as he stepped into the cubicle she called home.

"The doctor," he snapped at the girl who had guided him. "Run to the infirmary and get medical aid."

Alone he stooped over the narrow cot and the supine figure it contained. Devoid of her shielding cowl the old woman looked like a mummified corpse. The skull was bald but for a few wisps of straggling white hair, the skin crèped and looking like leather. The eyes opened as Dumarest touched the scrawny throat.

"Water! I thirst! Give me water!"

A plea couched in a whisper which he barely heard. A small table stood beside the bed containing a decanter of water, a glass, a small bottle of some volatile liquid. A few crumbs lay scattered on a scrap of brightly colored paper; the remains of a snack bought at one of the stalls.

Dumarest poured the glass half-full, sniffed at it, held it to the parched lips. She drank as he supported her, lifting her almost upright, laying her back as she finished the water.

"You shouldn't be alone," he said. "I've sent for help."

"Which I don't need—and my own company's good enough."

"I'll pay for it." Dumarest guessed the reason for her objections. Quietly he added, "Who put you up to it, Mother?"

"What?" Her eyes were suddenly bright, wary. "I don't know what you're talking about."

"Yes you do."

"No, I—" She licked her lips. "My head hurts and I've a burning in my stomach. Leave me. I must sleep."

"The reading," he said. "Reiza brought me to you, remember? Who told you what to say?"

"A reading? You want a reading?" Her hand fumbled beneath her pillow and returned bearing the familiar deck. "Shuffle. You have to shuffle."

Dumarest said, harshly, "Quit trying to con me. I've handled an arcana deck too often not to know when one has been stripped. The pack I shuffled was too thin. You'd selected the right cards and made the switch after I'd finished with them." He leaned closer to the withered face. "Who told you to do it? Who told you what to say?"

The skull-like head rolled a little as, again, Krystyna licked her lips.

"Water! God! I burn!"

Dumarest could feel the heat of her as he lifted the thin body with his left hand. Water dribbled from the glass over her chin, spattering as it fell to her chest.

"Help's coming," he said as he put her down. "The girl is getting the doctor." And taking too long about it or the man was hard to find. "Now tell me who gave you the orders."

"Orders?"

"About the cards." Dumarest forced himself to be patient. The woman, old, afflicted by what ailed her, could be finding it hard to concentrate. "The reading. Reiza brought me to you. Who arranged with you to make the switch?" A thing easily done in the guttering candlelight; cards placed on the pack he'd shuffled from where they'd been kept hidden in a wide sleeve of the robe. "Who told you what to say?"

"Eh?"

"Who told you what to say?" The important question, one he repeated. "Who told you what to say? Tell me, damn you! Tell me!"

She responded to the raw anger in his tone, trying to rise in the bed, gasping as he supported her. Cards riffled from the gnarled hands to lie in a scatter on the bed, the floor. One lay face-up on her chest. The depiction of an hourglass.

Time—for him it was running out.

"Krystyna!" Dumarest leaned over her, fingers searching, finding no movement beneath the dry texture of her skin. "Krystyna!"

She was dying, already dead, showing no sign of a pulse in neck or wrist. Dumarest lowered his hands, thrust his clenched fists hard beneath the breastbone in a series of impacts against the heart. As again he made to check her pulse the doctor burst into the cubicle.

"Here, let me!"

He was skilled, fast and efficient, working with drugs, a hissing hypogun, trained massage. For long minutes Dumarest could do nothing but stand and watch.

Then, as the doctor straightened, shaking his head, the girl who had followed him into the cubicle said, "Will she be all right now?"

"No, I'm afraid not. She's dead."

"Dead?" Her voice rose a little. "But she was just tired and wanted to rest for a while. How can she be dead?"

The doctor glanced at Dumarest then at the girl. Gently he said, "It happens, my dear. Krystyna was very old. She could have gone at any time."

"But—"

"There's no more I can do." At the door the doctor paused, turning to look back at the dead woman. "I'll send men to take care of things. The best thing you can do, my dear, is to get back to work."

To the booth and the anodyne of effort. Dumarest caught her by the arm as the girl headed toward the door.

"Do you know if she was close to anyone in the circus? Or if anyone had a hold over her?"

"Krystyna? No." Her eyes were moist, soon the tears would flow. "Everyone loved her."

"That food." Dumarest nodded at the crumbs and paper. "Did you bring it to her?"

"No." Her lower lip began to tremble. Her head turned from him, hands rising to mask the ruin of her face. "Let me go now. Please let me go!"

He heard the fading noise of her running feet and turned for a last look at the cubicle, the body it contained. One surrounded by the cards she had used, one still held in her stiffening fingers.

Dumarest pulled it free and looked at the coils, the raised head, the iridescent scales. The Snake—the symbol of lies.

CHAPTER NINE

Dumarest heard the roar from the crowd, the following, pregnant silence and guessed that Reiza was heading for the grand finale of her act. A moment of tension in which Chang would rear before her, poised with claws extended, then to drop, one paw lashing out, the razor claw shearing through the fabric of her halter to release the confined breasts.

A dangerous trick requiring split-second timing and fine precision but one the crowd loved. As the roar came again, men yelling their appreciation, Dumarest moved quickly beneath the stands. Next would come the clowns, then, the ring cleared, the final procession. A time in which the artists would be engaged as would most of the roustabouts, the musicians, Zucco himself.

The best time for him to act.

He pressed on, heading toward Shakira's private quarters, with a deliberate economy of movement. A man dressed in functional blue glanced at him, recognized him and turned away. A guard or technician and Dumarest passed two others. In a secluded corner he had chosen from previous examinations of the area he knelt and produced rags from beneath his tunic, a bottle of volatile spirit from a pocket, a package of chemicals from another.

Fire fumed from his hand, caught the spirit-soaked rags and leaped in consuming hunger. As it grew he threw the chemicals on the flame and, as smoke billowed in thick, dark clouds from the fire, rose and ran down a curving passage.

The fire was harmless; the plastic membrane would not burn

but it would sag and shrivel in the heat. A true blaze would have been dangerous, the smoke was merely to give the impression of a holocaust.

"Fire!" Dumarest shouted as he ran. "Fire! Fire! Fire!"

The smoke followed him, filling the air with an acrid stench and blocking vision. A man, running, cannoned into Dumarest and reeled to one side. Another cursed and dived back into a room. Within seconds alarms sounded, adding to the confusion.

But that would not last. Trained, the circus personnel would soon isolate the source of the smoke, deal with it, have things returned to normal. Bare minutes in which Dumarest had to complete his plan.

A door opened beneath his hand. A panel ripped open to reveal a mass of printed circuits. The knife in his hand lifted to slash across the complex tracery, sparks arcing, fretting the edge. Damage which killed the lights and he hoped would negate Melome's protection.

The forces which could kill him if Shakira hadn't lied.

A gamble and luck was with him. The girl rose from her chair as he burst into her room, mouth opening to scream. Sound muffled by the hand he clamped over her mouth.

"Sing and I'll kill you," he snapped. "Scream and I'll do the same." A meaningless threat but she wasn't to know that and he felt her sag in the circle of his arm.

A length of fabric was tucked under his belt, one bearing a knot the size of an egg. He thrust it into her mouth, tied the gag firmly behind her head, and lifting the slight body threw it over his shoulder. As he left the room he heard a peculiar wailing scream from deeper in the secluded area. Another which followed it and which could have come from no human throat. As it died a burst of maniacal laughter jarred his ears and dewed his face with sweat.

"Easy," said Dumarest as the girl stiffened under his arm. "I'm not going to hurt you. I'm just going to take you for a ride. A trip to town. Just relax now."

He ran down the passage and back into the smoke. Men, invisible in the reeking, chemical fumes, shouted above the hiss of extinguishing sprays. Dumarest avoided them, racing along a remembered way, reaching the rollers of an air-trap, thrusting his way through them and halting at the door beyond. It was locked, the catch yielding to the pressure of his blade with a snap of broken metal. As it swung wide he dived through it, slammed it shut and wedged it with a bin half-filled with a fibrous mass. The detritus of the filters above.

He raced past them, taking the stairs three at a time to reach another locked door at their summit. One which proved more stubborn than the last and he thinned his lips as he fought the catch. Time was against him. Already the fire must be under control, the ruse discovered and Melome missed. Unless he escaped soon he would not be able to escape at all.

The door yielded and he passed through to stand on the roof of the circus. All around reared the spires, towers, pinnacles of illusive spaciousness, the whole illuminated by the glow of the night sky. The starlight altered colors and he stood fighting to orient himself. That way? This? Beyond that minaret? That dome?

Long seconds in which he mentally reviewed what lay beneath the surface of the roof then, deciding, Dumarest loped over the firm covering. A twist, a turn and a long, curving convexity. A striped creation and there, nestling in a spot between rearing protrusions, he saw it. The raft he had stolen to reach the circus, apparently undiscovered and unharmed.

Placing the girl within its body he said, "Lie still now. Don't move and don't try to run. I'd rather not hurt you but unless you obey I'll knock you out. Understand?"

He saw her eyes, wide and terrified, limpid pools in the starlight. A creature tasting the terror she had so often aroused in others. One deserving of pity but his need was too great to allow of gentleness.

Dumarest swung himself into the raft and reached for the controls. They were slow to respond and he snarled, anger turning his face into the savage mask of a killing beast. Then the vehicle lifted, rising higher as he fed power to the antigrav units. Only when the circus had fallen far behind and below did he relax.

The girl stiffened as he touched her, gasped as he removed the gag.

"Don't sing," he said quickly. "Talk if you want but in a normal tone."

"What do you want of me?"

"You know what I want."

"But Tayu was giving it to you."

Dumarest said, harshly, "As and when he decided but it wasn't enough. I haven't the time to play his game."

"And you think I'll play yours?"

She had grown in more ways than one and Dumarest studied her in the starlight. A little more rounded and far more self-assured. She had called Shakira by his first name—how close had they become? How often had they talked and how often had he accelerated her growth? Each time she slept drugs could have shortened the months. Was he hoping to speed the development of her talent?

Dumarest said, "I need to find out one thing. When I have found it I'll have no further use for you. I'll give you money and you can go your own way. Return to the circus if that's what you want or move to another world. But I can't afford to wait."

"Because you are afraid?"

She paused then, as Dumarest made no answer, said, "You are afraid. But Tayu said it was a fear which made you strong. A challenge you'd accepted and, by accepting it, proved your courage."

"Did he tell you more?"

"The cause of your fear? No. But I think it has to do with something out there." Her hand lifted to point at the stars. "Something coming close."

Avro moved, a mind suspended in darkness as his body was immersed in the amniotic tank of his ship. A special vessel which he had used before when on a similar mission. The product of the Cyclan workshops and incorporating new techniques and discoveries which gave it an incredible velocity.

But, as fast as it was, for him it was still too slow.

Baatz was distant and Tron would be there before him. The cyber had been sent his orders and would obey them but the unknown factor could negate even the most carefully laid plan. If the agent proved less than reliable or made the fatal mistake of underestimating Dumarest. If an engine should fail or a generator develop a fault. If an animal should escape confinement and run wild in a killing frenzy—the possibilities were endless and, even though of a low order of probability, they had to be reckoned with. Only when Dumarest was safe and fast in his care would Avro be satisfied.

In the meantime he could do nothing but wait.

But to wait did not mean to be inactive.

Avro concentrated his mind. Already devoid of sensory irritations, it was only a moment before the Samatchazi formulae completed total detachment from reality. Only then did the engrafted Homochon elements become active. Rapport was immediate.

Avro expanded into something unique.

Each cyber had a different experience. For him it was as if he were a bubble moving in continuous motion in a medium of light interlaced with other bubbles. Minute globes which interspersed but never touched. Each, like himself, the living parts of an organism which stretched across the galaxy. All moving toward and coming from the glittering nexus which was Central Intelligence.

It absorbed his knowledge as if it were a sponge sucking water from a pool. Relaying orders in turn with the same efficiency. Mental communication which was almost instantaneous.

The rest was sheer intoxication.

Always, after rapport, was this period in which the Homochon elements returned to quiescence and the machinery of the body realigned itself to mental control. Avro drifted in a vast emptiness in which he sensed strange memories and unfamiliar situations; the scraps of overflow from other intelligences. A strange, near-telepathic affinity with things he would never see and men he would never meet.

A time of mental euphoria but, as he sobered, his mind pondered certain oddities.

The communication itself—had there been hints of illogic? Everything was proceeding as to the predetermined plan, but had he sensed a trace of irony? The disturbing suggestion of fanciful speculation?

Things unsuspected by any ordinary cyber but Avro knew what they did not. The degeneration of the brains which formed a part of the gestalt of Central Intelligence threatened the stability and very existence of the Cyclan. The rot had been checked, the affected brains reduced to atomic dust, but unless the basic cause was isolated and removed the degeneration would continue.

Had it already gone too far?

He concentrated, trying to isolate impressions, sifting through the mass of imposed data to find specific details. The disposition of agents revealed no fault but their placement was a matter of basic logic. The movement of ships with attendant instructions— why did Cyber Boyle need to go to Travante? A moment and he had the answer and with it a reassurance that the brains comprising the organic computer at the heart of the Cyclan was not at fault. And yet still the nagging doubt remained.

Avro moved, feeling nothing in his amniotic tank, likening his existence to those who had gone before. The fortunate ones now sealed in their capsules, minds released from all physical irritations, free to think, speculate, extrapolate—was boredom the answer?

A question answered even as thought; no intelligent mind could ever get bored while problems remained to be solved. Those presented by the Cyclan would be minor in comparison to the greater questions governing the basic construction of the universe.

Had they, as he suspected, drifted into the construction of their own frames of reference? Building universes based on subtle alterations of present reality? The degenerated brains, perhaps, their observed insanity had been classic examples of aberrated thinking. Or had they been judged by too harsh a standard? Destroyed without due thought?

Questions already considered and certain answers had been found but only Dumarest could provide the concrete proof. Once the identity of an encapsulated mind could be transferred to a host-body real communication could be established. That and more—each mind could enjoy a surrogate life. Reward heaped on reward; potential immortality in a succession of young and virile bodies.

Virile?

Why had he thought of that?

A body was a machine and it was enough that it be functional. Beauty, agility, grace, charm were all unnecessary components. Youth was desirable because it extended the period of useful performance. The rest had no place.

And yet?

Avro spun in his tank as his mind became suffused with burning images. The mountains. The crystalline glitter of nests. The sheen of wings and the glow of sunlight warming pinnacle and crag. The moonlight which bathed the world in a silver, nacreous glow. The stars. The rain and cloud and gentle winds. The taste of crisp, morning air. The smell of grass. The soft impact of another living, breathing shape.

Madness!

A roiling succession of images, memories, accumulated data which tore at his mind and stability. Frightening, bursting in a crescendo which left him limp and gasping like the victim of a vicious attack. As he had been a victim but his enemy had been himself and it had been a foe without mercy.

Avro closed his hand and hit the emergency button set in the palm of his glove. Waiting as the fluid was drained from the tank and attendants came to strip him and restore him to an awareness of true reality. They had aged, paying for scientific achievement with their disturbed metabolism, unprotected as Avro had been in his tank. He watched them leave and, alone, sat and pondered his future.

He would be eliminated—that had been obvious from the first. Marle was using him as a prop in the barely possible event of failure. Should he succeed and bring Dumarest back to Cyclan Headquarters he would still be eliminated. His task done he would be expendable and used as an example to others. In Marle's place he would do the same.

And, as a servant of the Cyclan, he should acknowledge the punishment deserved and accept it.

Instead he had used his persuasion to gain his present mission; arguments based on irrefutable logic but had his main motivation been only to serve?

Or had he wanted to survive?

He leaned back, closing his eyes, conscious of the quiver of the ship as it hurtled through space but unable to feel it. As he was unable to feel hate and fear and love. But once, as an angel, he had known a new and different world.

One filled with smells and music. With taste and touch and physical reactions. Of wanting in biological heat, of concern and, yes, of hate and anger too. Emotions which had been strange and disturbing in their mind-unsettling effect. Now, sitting, he wondered what it would be like to live continuously with such things. To know the insanity of emotion as against the calm exercise of logical reason.

And why, during the interrogation, he had minimized his experience.

A precaution, followed with basic instinct, applied with calculated skill. Waking he had recognized his danger and done his best to guard against it. Now he was a living proof of Marle's inefficiency but, alone, that wasn't enough.

He had to capture Dumarest.

To win the secret he held.

The one thing which would ensure his potential immortality.

And he would win it. The man was boxed in a trap which

would shortly be surrounded by a cage. It was only a matter of time before he would be held and the secret obtained.

And Avro would be the master.

He opened his eyes and again pressed the button set into the glove now lying beside him. It was time for him to return to the tank. There to drift and dream and anticipate the power to come.

Melome said, "Earl, I'm cold. You're flying too high and I'm cold."

Dumarest turned from the controls and looked at her. She sat huddled in the body of the raft, small, pale in the starlight, knees drawn up to her chest, arms wrapped around her body. Her eyes followed him as he rose and came close.

"Cold? But the night is warm."

"I'm still cold." Her tone was petulant. "Look if you don't believe me." She held out an arm and he could see the goose-pimples marring the smoothness. She shivered a little as he touched her. "Please! Can't we go lower?"

"We aren't that high."

"Then land and build a fire or something. I'm freezing!"

Landing would waste time and to build a fire would be to advertise where they were. Did she want that? Dumarest touched her again and felt the chill of her skin. To one side lay the clown's disguise he had discarded and he lifted the fabric and wrapped it around her slim body.

"It won't be long," he soothed. "Once we hit the town I'll buy you some hot food and some new clothes. Gems too if you want them. Just be patient."

"I'm still cold."

A child or a stubborn young girl. It was hard to tell for even if the body matured the mind still retained its youth. Yet she seemed mentally alert and he guessed she wanted to exercise her power. To reassure herself that she held some measure of dominance. An attitude he encouraged; to beat her down would be to lose her cooperation.

Beneath him the raft tilted a little and he adjusted the controls, leveling it against the thrust of a vagrant wind. Rising he tried for clearer air and looked behind as the altitude increased. If there was pursuit it was invisible; the rafts riding without lights and staying low so as not to occlude the stars. A fault he was making but he was unfamiliar with the terrain and to ride too low was to invite destruction.

"Earl!"

"All right, Melome. We're going down."

The upper regions held chill winds which held an edge and he dropped the raft to its former level. Hunched in the clown's disguise the girl remained silent and, struck by a sudden suspicion, Dumarest went to kneel beside her.

"Listen to me," he said. "Do you feel ill? Odd? In any kind of pain?"

"I'm just cold."

"Did Shakira ever tell you what would happen to you if you ran away? Did he?"

"No."

"Be honest now."

"I told you. Tayu was good to me. Better than that bitch Kamala. Better than you—he didn't make me freeze."

"It won't be for long."

Dumarest frowned as he returned to the controls. He'd gambled that Shakira's threat had been a bluff and it seemed he'd guessed right. The girl was further proof; if anything, the owner would have safeguarded his property but apparently he'd made no effort to hold her. Nor to follow her; even if rafts had raced ahead to town they would have no idea from which direction he'd arrive.

And yet it seemed too easy.

The raft tilted again and he evened its flight. Below, silvered by the starlight, he could see massed vegetation broken by rearing outcrops of stone. Jagged masses which could rip the bottom from the raft if they dropped too low and he lifted the vehicle to allow for any sudden change in the terrain.

"Earl! Can't we land? Walk around for a while?"

A good suggestion if the girl was really cold but not if she was hoping for rescue. Dumarest looked at the stars but failed to gain a clear direction. The points were too many and he had taken an erratic course since leaving the circus. The wise course would be to rise high in order to spot the lights of the town. To delay too long would be to risk missing it altogether.

"Hold tight," he said. "We're going up."

"Earl!"

He ignored the protest as he sent the raft rising toward the stars. Up, beyond the layer of chill winds, higher to where the air stung like knives, higher still as breath plumed from his lips and, behind him, the girl wailed her anguish.

And still he couldn't spot the town.

Something was wrong and he sensed it as he lowered the vehicle. The distance between circus and town wasn't all that great and with the distance he had covered and the altitude he'd gained the lights should have been visible. Instead he'd seen nothing but endless, silvered darkness.

Crouching, he fingered the wires behind the control panel, touching the steering control, the direction indicator. A simple gyro-compass but one which seemed to have unusual additions. He jerked free a wire and watched as the needle kicked across the dial.

From where she sat Melome said, "Is something wrong?"

"No."

A lie—Shakira had been smarter than he'd thought. The controls had been tampered with and, instead of heading toward safety, the raft had swung in a wide circle and was now level with or behind the circus. Dumarest sent it wheeling toward the left, straightened as he watched the needle, fed power to the engines as the vehicle cut through the air. A velocity increased as he tilted the nose, gaining the pull of gravity in a long, downward slope. One reversed as the silvered darkness came too close. An extended seesaw motion which would baffle any observer.

Melome whimpered as the air tore at her hair, the covering she held wrapped tightly around her.

"Lie down," snapped Dumarest. "Roll against the side and keep below the rail. You'll feel warmer out of the wind."

But the wind increased to a whining drone as he fought for speed to cover distance. To rise again as the ground loomed beneath him, to reach his apex, to dive again toward the rock-studded vegetation.

To double in agony as it came close.

The pain was a fire tearing at nerve and mind and sinew. One which struck without warning to blur his vision and turn the world into a hell of screaming torment. Dumarest sank, quivering, sweat dewing face and neck and body with a liquid film. A time in which he was helpless, conscious only of the agony which dominated every cell of his body.

Then, as Melome screamed, it eased to vanish as quickly as it had come.

"Earl! Earl!"

The raft leveled as he grabbed at the controls, juddering, metal grating from one side as it glanced off an upthrusting finger of stone. Then it was riding clear and Dumarest gasped for breath, tasting blood, aware of the jerking quiver of his hands.

The pain had gone—but why had it come at all?

Shakira?

He had gambled the owner had been bluffing—had he lost the wager?

For a long moment Dumarest kept the raft riding scant yards above the ground, eyes narrowed as he followed a clear path. Distance covered while he gained time to think and then, again without warning, the agony returned.

To send him doubled, writhing, the raft slewing to one side, the nose lowering to hit the ground, the rock half-buried within it.

CHAPTER TEN

There were rustles and squeaks and small scampering noises as rodents foraged in the vegetation. Sounds as harmless as the wind but which caused Melome to quiver in fear. Like most who clung to urban places, for her the open at night was filled with imagined terrors.

"It's nothing," said Dumarest. "Just the wind and creatures hunting for food. Small creatures," he added quickly. "Things like mice. There's nothing big or harmful on Baatz."

"How can you be so sure?"

"It's the air. It leads to pacifism. A predator needs to stalk and kill in order to survive. It can't do that if it just wants to lie down and dream."

A facile explanation but it had elements of truth and Melome relaxed, leaning back to look at the sky.

"I'm not used to the open. It's too big, too empty. You could get lost and wander and starve and die and no one would ever know." She shivered a little. "And it's cold."

The truth—the air held a pre-dawn chill. Dumarest paused in his task of gathering twigs and rose, stretching. Behind him the raft lay on its side, the nose crumpled, the controls useless. They had been lucky. The impact had flung them from the open body to land on cushioning fronds and, aside from minor bruising, neither was hurt.

"Earl?"

"We'll have a fire before long." He stooped and ripped free another mass. Most was green but enough had dried to feed a blaze. "Why don't you help? Pick some fuel and choose the lightest. Come on, now!"

She obeyed the snap in his voice and came toward him with a large bundle of fibrous strands. Dropping it she went for more while he arranged the fire, siting it before the raft so as to gain its protection against the wind. The open body would act as a reflector.

Fire winked as he stooped over a small heap of finely whittled twigs. It grew as he fed it with thicker pieces to steady into a red and glowing comfort topped by a rising plume of smoke.

"That's nice." Melome held out her hands to the warmth. She sat beside him, one shoulder touching his, the firelight touching the pale blondeness of her hair with dancing, russet glows. She looked less pale, more animated, her eyes holding a sharper expression. "Shouldn't you do something about the smoke?"

"No."

"They'll see it. If they come looking for us it'll guide them right here."

"I know."

"You want that?" She turned to look at him. "I don't understand. You stole me from Tayu and yet now you want them to find me and take me back to the circus. Why, Earl?"

He said, "The raft's wrecked and I don't know where we are. We've no supplies and this is hard country to make out in. Walking takes energy and we've no food to supply it. No water, either."

"So, unless they find us, we'll die. Is that it?"

"They'll find us."

"But I still don't understand why you stole me. I thought—" She broke off then, in a different tone, said, "I guess you just wanted me to sing for you. Is that it?"

The truth but he took his time admitting it. The firelight which gave her vivacity had also given her an unsuspected maturity. The pubescent girl had developed into a young and mature woman, one now touched by the magic of the night.

"Melome, I need—"

"I can give you what you need," she said. "I'm as much a woman as Reiza." Then, as he shook his head, "Why doubt it? Look at me. Touch me if you think I lie. Stop thinking of me as a child." She added, with a petulance which denied her claim to maturity, "Kamala kept me looking young. She thought a skinny girl would arouse sympathy and denied me certain things essential to my development. Tayu explained it all. I'm a certain physical type with a delayed pubescence but when it comes I catch up fast." The deep breath she took inflated her chest. "I've had drugs and hormones to help. Tayu wants me to be a real woman."

"Did he tell you why?"

"It's something to do with my talent. That or—" she shrugged. "Does it matter? I wanted to grow fast for you, Earl. Now you want to send me back."

"I've no choice."

"We could hide," she said. "Take a chance on finding our way. We might even spot another raft. One not from the circus. And I'll sing for you if you want. We'd be together and alone and I'll sing for you. Earl?"

He looked at her, a young, infatuated girl, and dangerous because of that. One who would deny him the use of her talent if he was curt in his rejection. Who could still withhold it should she doubt his intentions.

He said, "When you sing do you know what happens?"

"Those listening relive old terrors."

"But can you control the reaction?" He saw the shift of her eyes. "In a sense they move back in time," he said. "Become young again or not so young. Does the song govern that? And do you govern the song?"

"Earl! Look! A falling star!"

He ignored the arm she lifted, the finger she used to point at the bright streak against the sky.

"When you sang for me in the circus did you obey Shakira's orders as to how far to send me back?"

"Earl! Look! Another!"

She gasped as he caught her arm and turned her to face him. Her eyes widened as she saw his face, read his expression, the turmoil of his emotions.

"No! No, Earl! Please!"

A child caught in a web despite her protestations of maturity. Obeying orders, delaying him, keeping him locked in the prison of his own making.

One on which Shakira had turned the key.

The threat had been no bluff—the pain had proved that. Agony which had left him helpless and which would return should he attempt to escape. He remembered the card Krystyna had let fall toward the last. The Hourglass, the symbol of time.

How long did he have?

"Earl! Don't hurt me! Please don't hurt me!"

Who was the Snake?

"Earl!" Melome's voice rose as fear robbed her of confidence. Tears filled the luminous eyes and her lips trembled as he reached for her. "No! Don't! Please don't—"

She fell silent as his hand touched her hair, followed it over the curve of her head and shoulders. A soothing caress to which she responded, coming closer, resting her head against his shoulder as his arm closed around her shoulders.

He said, "You don't have to fear me, Melome. I'd never hurt you. I want you to believe that."

"I do." Her voice was muffled against his tunic. "It was just the way you looked at me. You were so savage."

"I was thinking of someone else."

"Tayu?"

"No."

"Zucco? Reiza?" Her voice took on a note of jealousy. "Who do you hate so much, Earl?"

"It doesn't matter."

"No," she said. "As long as it isn't me." She snuggled a little closer. "You're strong," she murmured. "So strong. I felt it from the very first. In the market when you made the deal with Kamala. I wanted to sing for you and then she told me. Well, you're here now and that's all that matters. Together we're safe."

"Yes." Dumarest fed more fuel to the fire. "Who else lives where you do in Shakira's private quarters? Have you seen them? Talked to them?"

"One. Elagonya's nice."

"What does she look like?"

"I don't know. I've never seen her. She wears a cloth over her head."

"Old? Young? How does she sound?"

"Like music. I asked Tayu about her once and he said she had a very special talent. He didn't tell me what it was but I think she makes dolls. I saw some in her room."

Dumarest said, "Did they look like anyone you know?"

"No, they were just dolls. Small, about that tall." Her hands measured a distance. "Some of them were very old."

"And her room, was it decorated with strange signs? Like those the fortune tellers used in the market."

"I didn't see any." Melome twisted in his arm to look at him. "Why so interested, Earl? What's Elagonya to you?"

"Nothing, but I knew someone once who made dolls. She tried to use them to hurt people."

"Not Elagonya." Her tone was emphatic. "She's too nice."

To her, perhaps, but to strangers she could be different. A sensitive, hidden away, unwilling even to reveal her face—what hatred could such a creature harbor against normal people?

"Earl, you're worried. I can tell it." Against him Melome stirred, relaxing as she yielded to the pressure of his arm. "Maybe I can help. Tell me why you're so worried."

"Forget it now. Just listen to the wind." It sighed as it caressed the silvered fronds, a susurration which filled the air. "And the crackle of the fire. It's like music, isn't it. And watch the stars. Perhaps more will fall. When one does you're supposed to make a wish. Did you know that?"

She muttered, sleepily, "Will the wish come true?"

"It might. So make sure it's a good one." His voice droned on, soothing, hypnotic in its comforting reassurance. He felt the weight of her slender body as she slumped against him, the sound of her deep, regular breathing. "Melome? Melome, are you asleep?"

A sigh was his answer and he fell silent looking at the fire, the smoke, the wheel of the paling stars.

The raft came two hours after dawn arrowing from the horizon directly toward the rising pillar of smoke. Dumarest watched it from where he lay buried in the vegetation far to one side of the fire. Melome, still asleep, lay where he had placed her close to the shelter of the wrecked vehicle.

She woke as the raft landed, rearing upright as Zucco strode toward her. He was tall, arrogant, wearing yellow and black, cruel colors which matched the expression on his face. The wand in his hand reached out, touched her arm, drew back as she screamed.

"Hurts, doesn't it, you bitch. Think of it the next time you're tempted to run from the circus. Where's the scum who helped you?"

"I didn't run! I—" She screamed again as the wand touched her body. "No! Don't hurt me! Please don't hurt me!"

"Where's Dumarest?"

"I don't know! I was asleep!"

"Where's Dumarest?" The tip of the wand hovered an inch from her face. "Why is he so interested in you? What can you do for him?" A sneer thickened his tone. "Aside from the obvious, that is. Talk, damn you! Talk!"

From where he sat at the controls of the raft Valaban said, "Take it easy, Jac. This isn't the way to handle the situation. The girl isn't to blame."

"Stay out of this!"

"I'm in it. Shakira—"

"Never mind him. I'm in charge and I don't intend wasting time. If you don't like it then you know what you can do." Zucco returned his attention to Melome. "Well, bitch, are you going to talk?"

"We crashed. I fell asleep. When I woke he had gone." Her arm waved at the surrounding vegetation. "He must have tried to make it on foot."

"In which case we can spot him." Valaban jumped down from the raft, staggered a little, regained his balance. "He must have left tracks and couldn't have got far. Let's load the girl and go looking."

"I told you to stay out of this." Zucco's voice was cold. "The next time you open your mouth I'll shut it for good."

"You could try." Valaban took a step closer, one hand buried beneath his blouse. "But it'll earn you a ruined face. I may be old and slow but this makes us equal." His hand appeared holding a flat gun, a twin to the weapon Reiza carried in the ring. "Now let's load the girl and lift. For all you know Dumarest could be within yards of us. Maybe hiding under the wreck and waiting his chance to jump us."

The truth but he had realized it too late. As he had guessed wrong as to the location. Like an animal, Dumarest had moved silently through the vegetation, taking advantage of the argument to get close, rising to lunge forward as Zucco turned to face the girl.

Valaban fell as Dumarest slammed against him, snatching the gun to level it as Zucco turned, snarling, the wand lifted in his hand.

"Drop it!" Dumarest fired as the man hesitated, the shot whining inches to one side of Zucco's body. "The next one you get in the face. Now drop that wand!"

He stepped forward as it hit the ground, thrusting back the

man with the heel of his left hand, the muzzle of the gun held steady in his right.

"Melome! Get up and get over here. Move!" He didn't look toward her as she obeyed. "Take hold of his hand, girl. Grip it tight."

"No. I don't want to touch him."

"He won't hurt you." Dumarest stepped back as he heard a rustle to his rear. "Stay out of this, Valaban. Move over to the fire and lie face down. And you," he snapped at Zucco as the old man obeyed. "Down and kiss the dirt."

"Go to hell!"

"You've a choice." Dumarest tightened his finger on the trigger. "You've three seconds to make it."

A moment and Zucco was down, lying with his face to the dirt, trembling with the helpless rage which consumed him.

"Right, girl, put your hand on his neck." A glance at his face and she obeyed. "Now sing, Melome. Sing!"

Dumarest jammed his hands against his ears as the air filled with the wailing cadences of her song.

It was different, driving through the bone and flesh and muscle of his hands, without the wail of pipe and pulse of drum and yet still it caught at his mind and sent it wheeling in a succession of phantom images. An effect lacking its true power because of the lack of contact. From where he lay beside the fire Valaban groaned and cupped his ears with veined and blotched hands.

Zucco lay as if dead.

A man lost in terror—a captive of the song.

Bound and helpless by the fantasies of his mind and suffering a greater punishment than any physical torment. Dumarest watched him and then, as Melome looked toward him, dropped one hand and sliced the edge across his throat.

An unmistakable signal and he lowered the other hand as she broke off her song.

"Into the raft, girl. Quickly!"

He followed her into the vehicle as Valaban sat upright, shaking his head. It rose as Zucco twitched, climbing as the man rolled over to sit with his face buried in his hands. Figures which dwindled as the craft soared into the sky.

"You did it!" Melome came to sit beside him. "You got us away."

"For now."

"You had it planned," she said. Her voice was excited; a

youngster enjoying a treat. "You left me asleep to act as bait and then, when they didn't expect it, you attacked. But what if there had been more?"

"Your song would have taken care of them."

"A weapon," she said. "You used it as a weapon. But I wasn't in contact so—" She answered her own question. "Zucco. You had him helpless. They would have had to obey." She laughed with pure delight. "Earl! You're so clever!"

Lucky would have been a better word. Had Zucco not given way to his spite, pandered to his sadism, the plan would have failed. As it could still fail.

Dumarest checked the controls. The raft was moving as it should in the direction indicated on the instrument but he sensed something was wrong. Why had Zucco come for them at all? Why had Valaban come with him? Any crew would have done and the circus had rafts and men to spare.

Questions lost in a sudden blast of pain.

As before it came without warning, a red tide of agony which doubled him over the controls and filled the universe with screaming torment. An eternity which lasted for seconds for when he could see again the raft was still on an even path, the ground below no different from what he remembered.

"Earl?" Melome was beside him. "Is something wrong?"

"Can you handle a raft?" A stupid question; how could she have learned. "Listen," he said urgently, "if anything happens. If I should fall sick, touch nothing. Understand? Stay away from the controls."

"Yes, Earl, but—"

The rest was lost as again fire caressed him, acid burned every nerve, vises crushed bones and sinew. A man flayed and set unprotected in the sun. As if smeared with honey and covered with ants. Boiled, broken, seared—all the torments ever devised inflicted in a wave of utter torment.

"Earl!"

Sweating, he reached for the controls. The escape had been an illusion, the trap Shakira had constructed still held him fast. More pain would come and more after that until he was helpless to do more than breathe. And Melome was in the raft, frightened, liable to do anything in her panic.

"Please, Earl, talk to me. What's happening?" She caught at his arm as the raft began to turn. "What are you doing? Where are we going?"

"To the circus," he said. "Back to Shakira."

He sat in his office of a dozen scents; odors and tangs echoing strange and alien places. Again he wore lavender, this time ornamented with a tracery of black which gave the appearance of somber scales.

"Be seated, Earl." A hand gestured toward the chair facing the wide desk behind which he sat. "I'm sure there is no need to warn you of attempted violence. You have had time enough to realize its futility."

Too much time. Hours during which he had been locked in a cubicle, given food, water, allowed to sleep after bathing. Time enough for Melome to be swallowed into the circus, for Zucco and Valaban to be rescued.

Dumarest said, "Why did you send them to recover the girl?"

An unexpected question and Shakira paused before replying.

"Someone had to go and they were best suited."

"An old man and a sadist?"

"Coincidence."

"No," said Dumarest. "Not coincidence but intent. Did you want them both out of the way at the same time? Or did you hope I would do what you seem to lack the courage to do?"

"And that is?"

"Zucco is ambitious. He yearns for power and intends to get it. Resents having to take orders. You are old. Need I say more?"

"You imagine he thinks of killing me and taking over the circus?" Shakira lifted his hands in the sudden, upward gesture. As he lowered them he said, "Do you really think it would be as simple as that? For a barbarian, perhaps, but we are not barbarians. There are considerations of finance, administration, loyalties, contracts. Those who work for the circus of Chen Wei would not be eager to follow a murderer. Would you?"

"If I had the choice, no."

"You are bitter," said Shakira. "You are thinking of the pain. The agony you had to bear as the price of your disobedience. But why blame me for that? I warned you what could happen and you chose to disregard that warning. Or you thought it a bluff. A mistake—I never bluff. Those who know me would have told you that."

"Reiza, for example?" Dumarest watched as Shakira made no movement. "Krystyna? Valaban? Helga, even? Melome? Who knows you, Shakira? Who really knows you? Elagonya? Your tame sensitive. Does she know what you are?''

"Shrewd," murmured Shakira. "I sensed it from the first. Shrewd and cunning and with a primeval instinct for survival which operates on an intuitive level. Which is why I was glad when you agreed to work for me.''

"Work," said Dumarest. "As yet I've done nothing but walk around and let myself be seen. You didn't want me for that.''

"You are wrong, but there is more.''

"What?''

"You will learn soon enough." Shakira rose and stepped from his desk. "But first let me introduce you to Elagonya.''

She sat in a cubicle thick with the fumes of aromatic incense but despite the pungent smoke the air held an acrid stench. One based on corrosive acids, alien exudations and warning odors. A blend which caught at his nostrils and Dumarest wondered why Melome hadn't mentioned it.

Shakira gave the explanation.

"You are a stranger," he said. "A hostile intrusion into her environment. For the sake of your life, I warn you not to be violent. Do not even think of extracting revenge. Before you could act you would be dead.''

"A telepath?''

"No, but with you she has a rapport. One built on fragments of your blood, tissue, muscle, bone. A focal point for her directed thought. Sometimes she incorporates it into a doll.''

Small artifacts which Dumarest could see lying around. Crude things with vacuous faces and oddly distorted bodies. The product of unskilled hands or hands so disfigured that they were incapable of normal dexterity.

"I found her on Tomzich, a world in the Bannerheim Cluster. She was living in a cave at the edge of a village living on scraps and hiding from the light of day. A mutant, hated by those from whom she had sprung. At times she cursed them and, at times, those cursed would die. They called her a witch and would have killed her had they been able." Shakira stepped forward and rested one hand on the rounded hump of a shoulder. "My dear," he said gently. "Have I your permission to reveal your face?''

The masked figure turned to face Dumarest, the covered head seeming to tilt as if to question.

He said evenly, "As you wish, my lady. Here, at this time, I am at your command.''

Shakira lifted the cloth.

Elagonya was a parody of what a woman should have been. The victim of cruel nature which, tormented by the blasting radiation which had distorted the pattern of genes, had taken a vicious revenge. The face was a jumble of features, one eye higher than the other, the mouth a twisted gash, the chin cleft so that it was forked, the nose the grotesque appendage of a clown. Lank hair hung like worms from a peaked skull and the eyes, muddy brown, flecked with yellow and red, looked like the dusty windows of an empty house.

"No surgery can aid her," said Shakira. "No drugs or treatment alleviate her condition."

It must have been a living hell. Dumarest looked at the warted encrustations on the skin, the puffed cysts marring the lines of the scalp. The gown she wore came high up the throat and covered the arms and legs to touch the floor but he could guess at the condition of the body it covered.

The whisper of her voice was the thin grate of a nail on slate.

"You look at me and do not cringe. Are you so accustomed to horror?"

"That is not what I see, my lady."

"You mock me?" For a moment tension stiffened the air and Dumarest heard Shakira's sharp inhalation, the touch of something like a feather against the naked surface of his mind. And then, as if he had been tested and had passed the test, the tension vanished. "No," she whispered. "You do not mock. Yet I do not need your pity."

"Something else, then?" A question to which she gave no answer and Dumarest continued, "We are what we are, my lady, and have no hand in our making. Therefore we should not be blamed for what we cannot help. Nor derided. Nor abused. But to deny pity is to reject what is good in a person. And there are those who, if they were you, would beg for more than pity."

"A quick and merciful end—you offer me that?"

"If I did, would you accept it?"

"No." The denial was sharp. "I live and while I live I serve. I can help those who have been kind." A sleeve lifted to reveal a knotted appendage which touched Shakira's hand. "Save your pity for those who need it. I do not."

Dumarest bowed, lowering his eyes.

"Yet you have been kind and merciful in your fashion. Tayu!" He lowered the cloth to hide the ravaged features, the fabric softening the harsh-timbre of the whispering voice. "Therefore, from me to you, something to remember."

The touch came again, a feather on the mind followed by a wave of pleasure so intense as to send his mind spinning in a vortex of indescribable ecstasy. One which blinded him to the journey back and left him shaken and gasping in Shakira's office.

"Her talent, Earl." The owner offered him a glass of wine. "The reverse of the coin she can spin at will. Pleasure and pain. Reward and punishment. Ironic, isn't it, that such power should be housed in such a frame."

The price paid by most sensitives for their talent; physical weakness and deformity, but Elagonya had paid higher than most. How many others like her did Shakira keep in his private quarters? And how to break the hold she had over him?

Dumarest said, "In order to function she needs a focal point."

"That is so." Shakira lifted his own glass of wine. "You had no choice but others are more cautious. Also her ability is limited." He sipped and swallowed and, looking at his glass, added, "I wanted you to realize how helpless you are, Earl. Run and pain will torment you. Attempt violence against me and you will be rendered helpless. Elagonya's talent has fabricated an affinity between you. In a sense you are an extension of her body."

"And?"

"That makes you mine, Earl. A part of the circus of Chen Wei."

CHAPTER ELEVEN

In a gallery a man was protesting, his voice high, edged with anger, "You cheated me! Sold me rubbish! That's bad enough but you took me for a fool. No one does that and gets away with it!"

"Easy, mister." The grafter, small, wizened, spread his hands in an age-old gesture. "There's no need for temper. You got what you paid for, right?"

"Wrong! A liquid which turns metal into gold—the damned stuff wears off after a day!"

And he had spent more than its cost in coming back to complain. An awkward one. A noise. He turned as Dumarest touched his arm.

"I'm an assistant market-inspector attached to the circus from the main office, sir." A lie the man was willing to accept especially when Dumarest continued, "As I see it you have a good case. You can prosecute or come to some settlement. Naturally we'd prefer you to prosecute; thieves like this mustn't be allowed to rob honest people. Are you willing to place charges?"

"Well—"

"Of course if you prosecute you'll have to attend court and pay certain charges which you can later claim against the defendant should the verdict go against him. And it will take some of your time. The preliminary hearing, the depositions, witnesses and their statements—naturally you have proof of purchase?"

"No." The man scowled. "Look, must I go through all that? It's time and expense I may never recover."

"You'd rather settle without formality?" Dumarest registered his disapproval. "Well, it is your right, of course, but hardly fair to others. But if that's the way you want it go ahead."

"A creep." The grafter scowled as the man, his purchase price refunded, moved away. "What the hell did he expect for a lousy kobold? Thanks for taking care of it, Earl."

"Forget it. How's trade?"

"Bad and getting worse. Why doesn't Shakira up stakes and move?"

"Ask Zucco—he's the one dragging his feet."

A suggestion he'd sown and which would spread like wildfire and if it created discord between the owner and the ringmaster Dumarest would be satisfied.

The gallery ended and he entered another familiar in its scenes of torture and pain. A woman stood before a tableau dimmed with shadows which shrouded the depicted figures in brooding menace. Tall, robed figures in scarlet watching the victim as he strained against his bonds. One lying supine on a bench, face contorted, bulging eyes fastened on the razor-edge of the curved blade swinging above him. A pendulum which lowered by degrees until it would slice through skin and fat and flesh and inner organs.

"Horrible!" She shuddered as Dumarest halted beside her. "The things people imagine! Could a thing like that really have happened?"

Too often and in too many places and he said so, not softening his words.

"But those men. They're cybers. The Cyclan doesn't operate like that."

"Those aren't cybers."

"No?" She turned to face him and Dumarest saw the glint of amusement in her eyes, the quirk of lips artificially enhanced. A matron on the prowl knowing the erotic stimulus of depicted agony and willing to respond to any advance he might choose to make. "They look like them."

"What do you know of the Cyclan?"

"Me? Not much but I've a cousin who tried to join them. That was on Pikodov—my home world. Then I married and we settled here. A mistake, I was widowed within five years."

"And Juan?"

He was really involved. That's how I know what they look like. Cybers, I mean. One used to come to the house to give initial instruction or make tests or something. Odd me seeing these." She gestured at the tableau. "I saw one only this morning in town."

"A cyber?"

"That's right. At the Dubedat Hotel. I'm staying there." Her voice was suggestive. "A big room and I'm all alone and I hate not having company."

"If I'm free we'll have dinner tonight," said Dumarest. "Had the cyber just arrived?"

"No. Someone told me he'd booked in a day or so ago."

When he'd run with Melome from the circus. When Zucco and Valaban had been sent after him. Coincidence—or design?

A question Dumarest pondered as he moved on to the shadowed area beneath the stands. It was between performances, the ring holding the dilapidated, slightly tatty air such places always did when the lights dimmed and the stands were empty. Some men raked the sand, smoothing and cleaning the surface while others worked in the tiers. Routine tasks which would soon be completed.

Citizens of a world of which Shakira had made him a part.

A close, snug, normally safe world but a prison to a man used to the spaces between the stars. Dumarest moved on, conscious of the partitions which reared too close, of passageways too narrow and ceilings too low. They lifted as he moved deeper beneath the stands but still the sense of confinement remained. That and the warning prickle of danger which he had learned never to ignore.

"Hi!" Valaban lifted a hand in salute as Dumarest came toward the cage in which he stood. "Be with you in a second, Earl."

He stooped over the limp body of a feline, hands deft, fingers probing, grunting as he jerked a splinter from the thick, black fur. A slender shaft, pointed, tipped with a tuft of wool at the thick end.

"Nice." He handed it to Dumarest and slammed shut the cage. "Some bastard wanted a little fun and used a blowpipe. I've warned Reiza about that trick of hers but she won't listen. She'd be crazy to try it anywhere else."

Dumarest turned the dart in his fingers. "Do you get much of this?"

"Not on Baatz. Other worlds are different. You'd think people would have more sense but they want more than entertainment. They want blood."

"Maybe they should be catered to," Dumarest handed back the dart. "Fights," he explained. "Open bouts and championships. Mixed pairs, even. Bets on first blood, third or to the death. There's money in it. I'm surprised you aren't running them."

"Shakira wouldn't hear of it."

"How about Zucco?"

"Maybe, but Zucco isn't the boss." Valaban looked at the limp body in the cage. "But he's good at his job. He saw the cat twitch and gave the signal without delay. Before it could jump the clowns went in with gas and knocked it out. It'll recover soon."

"And Reiza?"

"Lucky—but mad as hell."

"About the cat?"

Valaban hesitated then said, "Look, Earl, maybe it's none of my business but it wouldn't do any harm for you to be careful. When we got back she spent some time with Zucco. They were talking and she didn't like what he said. I guess you haven't seen her since you left?"

"No. I've been busy."

"And she's been alone. Thinking, brooding—remember what I told you about cats and women? You can't trust either. And she's handy with that whip."

Too handy. Dumarest felt the bite of it as he turned. The raw sting as again the lash touched his cheek.

Facing him Reiza said, "You bastard! This time you lose your eyes!"

She wore a gown of yellow edged with black, draped so as to bare one shoulder, belted at the waist, the fabric taut over the mounds of her breasts, the swell of her hips and thighs. A garment designed to enhance her femininity but there was nothing soft or gentle about her face or eyes. It was the mask of a tiger illuminated by the narrowed, blazing slits of rampant jealousy. Her voice carried the echo of the crack of the whip she held in her right hand.

Backing, Dumarest said, "Reiza! Be careful!"

"Like hell I'll be careful!" The lash tore the air before her. "I trusted you! Wanted you! Loved you more than I'd ever loved anyone before. And you run off with that pallid freak. Spent the night with her under the stars. How was she, Earl? Did you lie to her too? Tell her you loved her? Use her as you used me!"

He said, "Reiza! Shut up and listen!"

"I've listened to all I want. I've heard how you were found snuggling close. How she clung to you and cried when you parted. The state she was in. You dirty swine! You filth! To prefer that bitch to me!"

Jealousy bordering on madness. Dumarest dodged as the lash tore at his face, feeling the wind of it, the heat of its passing. Leather moving at supersonic speed and able to slice flesh as if it had been a knife. To kill a fly without disturbing the sweat it was drinking—or to tear out an eye as a man would thumb a pea from its pod.

A threat he had faced before and from the same source but now there was a difference. Then she had been playing, teasing him as a cat would tease a mouse, enjoying the game and the demonstration of her skill. Now she wanted to hurt, to maim and blind—and she had the ability to do it.

"Reiza, listen to me." Again Dumarest dodged, the whip slicing the plastic of his tunic at one shoulder. "Damn you, woman, listen! To Valaban if not to me. He was there. He'll tell you what he saw."

"I know what he saw. If he says different he'll be lying. You were with that girl. That freak Melome. You slept with her. You chose her over me. Me!"

A woman too much like a cat. One who had suffered imagined insult and who now wanted nothing but a savage revenge.

Dumarest backed as the lash whined toward his face, felt the bars of the cage slam against his spine, moved quickly to one side the thong hitting metal. A grab and he had it in his hand, a twist and it was around his knuckles. A moment in which each faced the other as she pulled and then, with a sudden jerk, he had thrown her off balance, to stagger, to trip over his foot, to sprawl in an ungainly heap on the littered floor.

She screamed in fury as he slammed his foot hard on the hand holding the whip.

"Jac! Kill him, Jac! Kill him!"

Dumarest stooped, snatched up the whip and rose with it in his hand. Zucco stepped from the shadows as he turned, tall in his ringmaster finery, his own whip lifted before him. One he lost as Dumarest sent his lash against the tall stock, ripping it from the other's grasp and sending it flying to one side.

"Jac!" Reiza almost sobbed in her rage as she rose to her feet, one hand nursing her bruised wrist. "Kill him! Kill him and I'm yours!"

"You have always been mine." Zucco looked at Dumarest. "Do you understand, you poor fool? She went with you for a whim. A momentary passion which I permitted for reasons of my own. Later, perhaps, we shall laugh at your ineptitude."

"As you laughed at Hayter's death?" Dumarest saw the cold, sneering mask of the ringmaster change a little. "You did kill him, didn't you? You wanted the woman that badly. So you made sure he carried a scent which would turn the cats into a fury. The act of a coward—but what else are you?"

"Your better," said Zucco tightly. "Your superior. Now and at any time."

"As you demonstrated in the sump." Dumarest shrugged and half-turned toward Reiza, the whip dangling in his hand. "If you want revenge," he said, "pick yourself another champion. Only a man has the guts to fight for a woman he wants. Zucco hasn't got what it takes."

"You think not?"

"He's a murderer, a liar, a cheat and a thief. Things once said about me. Maybe the accusation holds an element of truth. But I'm not a coward."

"Neither is Jac." Reiza looked at Zucco. "Please, don't shame me. Kill him and take me in any way you want—but kill him. Kill him!"

"He can't," said Dumarest. "Not in the open. Not when I'm unchained and he hasn't got a gun and some bullies like Ruval to back him up. Scum like Zucco work in the dark with poison and hired assassins. Take him for what he is if you want him so badly. Let him own you, use you, beat you as he wants. But never make the mistake of thinking him a man."

Her laughter surprised him. "You think that? You believe him helpless? Afraid? Jac!"

"A challenge," he said, and smiled, standing relaxed, arrogant in his confidence. "Us facing each other on equal terms.

Armed with knives and battling to the death. Is that what you have in mind?''

From where he stood Valaban said, urgently, ''Don't listen to him, Earl. Don't let him goad you. Let him have the bitch and good riddance. She isn't worth fighting over.''

''Shut up, you old fool!'' Reiza snapped her anger. ''Stay out of this.''

Dumarest ignored them both. To Zucco he said, ''I don't fight for nothing. If we meet what is the prize?''

''The girl. I win and she is mine. If you beat me—''

''I gain nothing,'' said Dumarest. ''I don't want her.''

''The pleasure of killing me then—if you can.''

''I can do that now.'' Steel glimmered as Dumarest jerked free the blade from the stock of the whip he held. ''In fact I'd be a fool not to. So—''

''No!'' Shakira stepped forward from where he had stood watching from the shadows. He wore emerald traced with silver, ornamentation which caught and reflected the light to clothe him in the semblance of shimmering scales. Gleams Dumarest had spotted before Zucco had made his challenge. ''There will be no murder. A fair fight is another matter.''

Dumarest shrugged and lowered the blade. ''Why give an enemy the chance of killing you?''

''You think he could?''

''All fights are gambles.''

''And all gamblers need a wager. For what would you risk your life?''

''Unlimited access to Melome,'' said Dumarest. ''The end of a certain inconvenience. Money and freedom to travel and medical aid should I need it. The aid to be given without charge.''

''Agreed. And for you.'' Shakira turned to Zucco. ''What you have always wanted. The control of the circus of Chen Wei.''

''And me,'' said Reiza. ''In any way you want.'' Then, to Dumarest, she said, ''Think of that when he's killing you.''

''You're sure he can do that?''

''I'm certain of it.'' Her voice was high, triumphant. ''You're a fighter, Earl, but so is Jac. He was a champion before he joined the circus—and he bears no scars!''

Valaban filled his palm with a pungent oil and, as he rubbed it over Dumarest's naked torso, said, ''This is crazy, Earl. I tried to warn you. Why the hell didn't you listen to me?''

"How good is Zucco?"

"You heard Reiza." Valaban rubbed harder. "The bitch," he said bitterly. "I tried to tell her he was lying but she wouldn't listen. She didn't want to listen. Just like a cat. You think you own one then it up and leaves for someone else. No loyalty. No gratitude."

"She was upset."

"Sure, but would a normal woman have acted that way? At least she'd have given you the chance to explain. She didn't even turn a hair when you mentioned Hayter. Did you notice that? It's my guess she's known all along. Maybe that's what attracted her to Zucco—a pair of animals together. Well, to hell with her. Just watch out for yourself." Valaban scowled at the noise coming from the seats beyond the tunnel. "Listen to them! They should be in a cage!"

They filled the rows closest to the ring, cramming tight for the sake of a better view. Entrepreneurs abandoning their concessions, grafters, dancers, spielers, shills all able and willing to relinquish a profit for the sake of witnessing a bloody entertainment. And others from the circus proper; roustabouts, artists, clowns, technicians. Their voices droned like a swarm of bees.

Dumarest watched them from the mouth of the tunnel as he wiped his body free of surplus oil. A trace remained on his hands and he stooped to rub them in the sand; oil which would prevent an opponent from getting a hold had no place on fingers needing to grip a hilt. Straightening he heard a shout and saw Zucco step from the mouth of a tunnel opposite.

"Right, Earl," said Valaban. "I guess this is it. Go out and gut the bastard!"

A sentiment echoed in a roar as Dumarest stepped into the ring.

One he had heard too often before.

The cry of a beast scenting blood, mindless, unthinking, eager only to witness battle and agony. To see the spurt of crimson, the writhing of lacerated flesh, the screams of the maimed and dying, the final convulsions. To know the euphoria of vicarious combat. To bet and gloat if they won and to curse the vanquished if they lost.

A sound as familiar to Zucco as to himself.

Dumarest knew it as the man came forward, naked aside from shorts, his body bearing the sheen of oil. He ignored the crowd as he trod the sand, smiling, eyes narrowed as he summed up the opposition. And Reiza had told the truth—Zucco bore no scars.

The sign of a novice or of a victor who had never known the ice-burn of a razor's edge. One too fast to be touched, too deft, too cunning. An unmarked champion. A thing so rare as to be almost unknown and Dumarest wondered how Zucco had managed it. Bribes, fixes, special blades which oozed red but did not cut could provide a show and safety for those involved. Things common in booths where men offered to fight all comers for cash or put on spectacles for gaping yokels. But the cognoscenti of the arena would never be so easily deluded—and no man could become a champion without their support.

"You fear." Zucco halted, facing Dumarest, the space of yards between them. "I can smell your sweat. Yet the crowd is with you." His smile turned into a sneer. "Let them shout— soon they will have cause to regret their mindless braying. As you will have cause to regret your temerity."

Dumarest made no comment, standing poised on the balls of his feet, ready to move in any direction. Zucco seemed more at ease, relaxed, the knife in his right hand hanging at his side. Ten inches of curved and pointed steel, burnished to a mirror brightness, honed and tempered to cut through bone. An inch longer than Dumarest's own blade but it was one he was accustomed to and this was no time to change.

"Yield," said Zucco. "I give you the chance. Throw down your knife and admit defeat. Better to serve than to die and, if you obey, I'll let you have the woman."

"Does she know that?"

"What she knows or wants is of no importance. Soon I shall be the master. Then—"

He broke off as Dumarest lunged, darting to one side, his blade rising to clash against the one Dumarest thrust toward him. An open attack and an easy feint but the speed at which Zucco acted was illuminating. As was the quick move he made to one side away from a second attack.

"You are impatient, my friend." His smile held no humor. "And clumsy, too—your attack had no grace. A tyro would have done as well. I wonder you managed to survive so long."

"Talk," sneered Dumarest. He stumbled as he moved to one side, as clumsy as Zucco had said. "Is that how you win? Bore your opponents to death?"

"No." Zucco crouched a little, knife held forward like a sword, point slanted upward. "I cut them, my friend. I slash their veins to make them bleed and their tendons so as to leave them crippled. I blind them and watch as they grope in the dark. I nick their jugulars and hamstring them and, at times, I ruin them as men." The point dropped, darted toward Dumarest's groin. "I offered you mercy—now I shall teach you the meaning of pain."

He came with a flash of steel, metal ringing as Dumarest parried, attacked in turn, his own blade swept aside as Zucco diverted the cut to slash in turn.

An exchange which left Dumarest with blood streaming from a gash on his side and the crowd, roaring, on its feet.

"First blood to me." Zucco bared his teeth in a smile. "And a taste of what is to come. Don't delay, my friend. Show your admirers how skilled you are. See? I offer you a target."

He spread his arms to expose his body, still smiling, light catching the blade he held and turning it into a gleaming star. A man radiating a supreme confidence and Dumarest searched for the reason why.

Zucco was quick, lithe, agile, moving with a dancer's grace. Things essential to any good fighter but not enough on their own to account for his victories. His lack of scars. There had to be something more.

"You're cautious, my friend." Zucco lowered his arms. "Too wary to take what was offered. A pity. But why don't you attack?"

A question to match the invitation and Dumarest sensed he was close to the answer. To attack was to precipitate the action, to score if the attack was fast enough and the opponent slow. To force his reaction if neither and so to still retain the advantage. One lost if the party was unexpected and the return unusual. But if both could be predicted?

Dumarest weaved, slowly, edging forward, knife a gleaming sliver in his hand. It turned so as to catch and reflect the light, to catch the eye and to narrow the concentration. Tricks Zucco must know but even so his head moved as he followed the blade. Moved then steadied as Dumarest lunged in a feint, drew back, lunged again, the blade in his hand sweeping up and forward in a thrust which would have opened the other's abdomen had it struck home.

A gamble lost and he felt the lack of resistance, following the lunge with a blur of speed as Zucco struck in turn.

Again the crowd roared at the sight of blood.

"Fast," said Zucco. "The fastest I have ever met. Slower and you would be screaming from the pain of a severed kidney."

Instead the blade had struck low to bathe Dumarest's thigh with a carmine flood.

A wound far less serious than it looked but he played up to it, limping, nursing the leg as he faced the other man, who now seemed too reluctant to attack and, suddenly, Dumarest knew the reason why.

"So you've guessed." Zucco edged forward, losing his smile. "Not that it will do you any good. In fact it will add spice to the combat. To know that you are without a defense. That your skill is useless and it is only a matter of time before you are reduced to a whimpering parody of a man. Here, in this arena, you've met your master."

A telepath.

Zucco's special skill which Shakira had mentioned. A man who could read thought and intention and act before they had been turned into movement. A fighter against whom there could be no calculated defense.

Dumarest inched forward, accelerated into a lunge, darted to one side, feinted again, heard the clash of metal and felt the burn of steel. A cut on his upper arm, shallow, harmless, but a demonstration of Zucco's power. Another followed, the point aimed at an eye missing to nick an ear, Zucco following the blow to cut again as Dumarest turned.

"Soon," he promised. "Then the game will be over. I shall cut deep and hard—try to guess where and when."

Thoughts Zucco could read and so direct his attack. A man facing a threat could avoid it in only so many ways but before action there had to be thought and Zucco would know the decision. As he would be able to anticipate the nature of any offensive.

"Come," he urged. "Why delay? The crowd are for you. They want you to win. Don't disappoint them. Even a whining coward would have the guts to try."

Taunts followed by others all of which Dumarest ignored. An old trick aimed at blinding him with rage but he had met it too often for it to have effect.

Why did Zucco want him to attack?

"Come," he said again. "It's time you made up your mind."

Time?

Time!

Dumarest stooped, snatched up a handful of sand, flung it at the other's face as he darted forward. A blinding shower rendered harmless as Zucco moved aside. Moving again as Dumarest followed the grit with a handful of blood. Then he was within reach, his knife a shimmering blur, cutting, slashing, a thin, high ringing filling the air as the blades clashed, parting to strike again in a fury of action.

Action too fast for thought, born of the reactive instinct honed by numberless combats and augmented by Dumarest's natural speed. The speed was too fast for Zucco to follow and he backed across the ring toward the tunnel where Valaban stood, Reiza at his side, Shakira a shadowy figure behind.

"No!" Zucco backed faster, face distorted with terror as he read the grim, unrelenting purpose in Dumarest's mind. "No!"

Steel clashed as he parried, a thin red line marring the smoothness of his torso, another gaping just below the throat to add its carmine stream to the smears staining the chest and stomach. Blood stained the shorts and laced the oiled flesh.

"No!" Zucco screamed as again he felt the ice-burn of shearing metal. A shallow cut to join the rest but the wound to his self-confidence was far deeper. "Dear, God—no!"

A man facing death, knowing it, feeling the terror he had so often induced in others. His nerve broke as again Dumarest sent his blade to cut a furrow in the oiled skin.

He would be flayed, crippled, maimed, blinded—things Zucco could read in in Dumarest's mind. A mind without mercy, cold in its determination, maintaining a single red image as his body moved on an instinctive level, robbing Zucco of his advantage.

Turning he ran toward the mouth of the tunnel, screaming as Dumarest reached him, gripped his hair, turned him to stand, face tilted upward, the point of his knife at the straining throat.

"Talk," snarled Dumarest. "Talk!"

Before he sent the blade upward, the point slicing through skin and fat and tissue. Driving up through the lower jaw, through the tongue, up into the palate, the sinus cavities, the brain itself.

A slow and lingering way to end.

"No," said Zucco. "Don't." He was helpless, his own knife lying where he had thrown it on the sand, already, in imagination, feeling the slow thrust of the threatening blade. "No," he said again. "It's not what you think. I—"

He broke off, rearing, eyes wide, the sudden convulsion racking his body causing his spine to arch in a bow, which snapped forward to send his head down, driving his throat hard against the needle point of Dumarest's knife.

CHAPTER TWELVE

Reiza said, "You murdered him! Murdered him—you bastard!" She faced Dumarest in the tunnel, radiating her fury. An emotion which distorted her face and made it ugly. "He was unarmed, helpless, at your mercy. Begging, even, I saw his face. And you killed him. Butchered him!"

"No," said Valaban. "He committed suicide. Shoved his own throat against the blade."

"Liar!"

"If you say so." Valaban shrugged. "What does it matter? The right man died."

"You filth! Jac was murdered!"

"Yes," said Dumarest. "He was. But not by me." He held out his clenched left hand, turning it, opening it to show the dart resting on his palm. A sliver of wood tufted at one end the point dark with blood. "This did it. I took it from his body."

Outside there was noise as the crowd, the entertainment over, moved back to work. Already Zucco's body had been removed, attendants racking the sand and hiding the soil of combat. But in the tunnel it was quiet, a silence broken only by the restless padding of the feline Valaban had treated. Recovered now from the gas and sensing the tension.

Dumarest allowed that tension to grow as he stood, saying nothing, the dart on his palm. Reiza had backed away to stand beside Valaban. Dim gleams from the shadows revealed where Shakira stood, watching. Aside from them the area was deserted.

Then Valaban gave a curt laugh. "So someone put a dart in him. I'd say, Earl, you had a friend in the crowd."

"A handy thing to have. But why did he wait so long?"

"Who knows? Maybe Zucco was moving too fast. Or you were figured to win. Or—hell, pick your own reason."

"I have." Dumarest tossed the dart into the air and watched as it fell to the floor. "Zucco wasn't hit earlier because he was too difficult a target. Whoever fired that dart had to wait until he came close. Almost here to the tunnel, in fact."

"But that's crazy! You had him at your mercy—why should anyone want to hit him then? You didn't need any help."

Moving forward Shakira said, "What you're saying, Earl, is that someone here fired that dart."

"Yes."

"Who?" Reiza was loud in her demand. "Who killed Jac? What kind of filth would murder a helpless man?"

"You, perhaps."

"Me?"

"A woman scorned," said Dumarest. 'You turned against me because you thought I'd been with Melome. Maybe you heard what Jac told me in the ring or maybe he'd told you earlier. To him you were nothing. You could have realized that and remembered what happened to Hayter and why. Or perhaps you were promised more than he could offer."

"I'm no harlot!"

"You helped him. You took me to Krystyna for the reading after he'd told her what to say. Things he'd learned in the sump when he amused himself with that wand." Dumarest's voice thickened with anger at the memory. "He acted too bold for him to be wholly what he seemed. Knew too much for a man in his position. In the ring, after I discovered the truth about him, things fell into place. But something didn't fit. There was no need for Krystyna to die."

"She was old," said Reiza. "It was a natural death."

"She was poisoned." Dumarest was blunt. "Someone gave her a snack with an added content. A generous gesture from someone she had reason to trust. A mistake, as was killing Zucco."

Valaban said, "No mistake, Earl. He was killed in order to save your life."

"No. He was killed to shut his mouth."

"That's ridiculous!"

"Zucco could have killed me at the first engage," said Dumarest. "He knew I was going to attack and how. He could have struck home but instead he merely parried. A good fighter, even an expert one, would never have taken such a chance. The job is to kill fast and have done with it. To do otherwise is to invite disaster."

"Are you saying Jac wasn't a good fighter?" Reiza snapped the question. "He was a champion."

Now he was dead; a thing Dumarest didn't mention. Instead he said, "Zucco was playing with me. As a sadist he couldn't help himself. He wanted to see me sweat, hear me beg. That's why, when he was cut, he didn't cut too deep. He wanted to savor every moment while keeping to his contract. From his point of view it was a good one. I was to be crippled but not killed."

"Why?"

"Isn't it obvious?" Dumarest met her eyes. "I would be helpless, drugged, neatly wrapped and stored for later collection. Zucco would have his fun, his revenge, you and control of the circus. A pity it didn't work out that way. From your point, that is, you would have made a fine pair."

"The best!" She drew in her breath, chest heaving. "He was right—I was always his woman!"

Dumarest shrugged.

"It's the truth!" Her voice rose with the need to emphasize the statement. Behind her, in its cage, the great cat ceased its pacing and halted, glaring with baleful eyes. "You were an incident, a momentary madness, just as he said. A novelty which quickly palled. You and that freak! Jac would never have looked at her. He was my kind of man."

"Then why did you help to kill him?"

"I didn't!"

"You helped the one who did. Who gave you that snack to take to Krystyna?"

"It was harmless! Val—" She broke off and turned to glare at the old man. "You!"

"Shut up, Reiza!"

"You gave it to me. Her favorite, you said. Bastard! You killed her!"

"As he killed Zucco," said Dumarest. "With a dart. One like that he fired at your cat. Remember?"

She screamed in a sudden convulsion of rage, rearing, seeming to arch her back, spitting like one of the cats she knew so well. A reactive gesture as was the extension of her hands, the fingers curved into claws. The polish on her long, sharp nails gleamed like metal.

"Back!" Valaban circled, eyes wary, his left hand slipping beneath his tunic. "Get away from me, you bitch!"

"You killed Jac! Murdered him! For that I'll have your eyes!"

She exploded into action as a feline would attack, springing forward, hands outstretched, the rake of her nails furrowing the old man's cheek. He jerked free his hand as he gained distance, leveled the flat gun, fired as again she went for his eyes. The blast caught her in the chest. The second turned her face into a bloody jelly.

"Freeze!" The gun swung toward Dumarest, to Shakira, back to Dumarest again. "You saw what happened. She attacked me. I had no choice but to shoot."

"You still have no choice." Dumarest inched forward, the knife in his right hand lifting, circling so as to make Valaban turn toward him, his back to the cage holding the watchful cat. "But if you kill me the Cyclan will make you pay."

"So you know. Well, it makes it easier." Valaban lifted his right hand, the small tube it contained aimed at Dumarest's torso. "I won't have to kill you. The dart this contains will knock you cold for twelve hours. When you wake Tron will have you and I'll be rich."

"The circus," said Dumarest. "All of it. The help and backing of the Cyclan. Rejuvenation, maybe, the chance of a new life. What else did they promise?"

"Enough." The tube moved a little. "Don't try it. I know your speed. Drop that knife. Now!" Valaban relaxed a little as the blade hit the floor. "Good. You show sense. Not like that stupid cow." He glanced to where Reiza lay huddled. "She didn't have to die but maybe it's better she did. A clean start."

"Clean," said Dumarest and looked at the woman. His voice changed as he said, "But she isn't dead. She—"

He moved as Valaban turned his head, hurling himself forward, one hand hitting the floor, coming up with the knife he had dropped, throwing it in an overarm movement.

A bad throw; the blade spun, glittering, without true direction or force. A harmless distraction but Valaban responded to the threat of edge and point. He backed, slammed into the cage—and turned as sickle claws lashed through the bars in a blur of fur and fury.

Razor talons which caught his face just below the hairline, ripping down to strip the flesh from the bones, to leave a carmined skull in which rolled agonized eyes and the grinning parody of a smile.

Shakira lifted his glass and, looking at the wine it contained, said thoughtfully, "Who would have guessed the old man had so much blood?" Then, to Dumarest, he added, "I read that in a book once. Or something like it. It was a long time ago now and I wonder why I should remember it. But it seems apt."

Too apt for comfort and Dumarest tried not to remember the screaming thing lying in a pool of its own blood. The silence which came when severed arteries had ceased their spurting had signaled a merciful end.

"You knew," said Shakira. "But how? Zucco I could understand but Valaban? He seemed so harmless." He took a sip of his wine and smiling, said, "It would have been more logical to have suspected me."

"I did." Dumarest was blunt. "But you aren't that stupid. Only a fool or a sadist would warn a victim of his knowledge and Zucco was both. He couldn't resist having his little joke using Reiza and the cards. Valaban wanted Krystyna dead because she could lead me to Zucco and he would betray Valaban. Odd how both wanted the same thing."

"Zucco I suspected," admitted Shakira. "He was too ambitious."

"Which is why you wanted me to fight him. The only way you could defeat him—his telepathic ability had you cornered had you tried anything else." Dumarest took a sip of his own wine. "You took a chance there. I could have lost."

"As I told you, I'm an expert at assessing a person's skill. Zucco was a champion only because he'd never met a man of your caliber. A true survivor in every sense of the word. But Valaban?" Shakira shook his head. "He seemed so contented."

"A pauper in a small kingdom." The wine was rich and pungent and Dumarest held it in his mouth before letting it trickle down his throat. The combat was over but the battle had still to be won. Twelve hours, Valaban had said. How long did he really have? "He betrayed himself in small ways. No man who'd worked for the circus as long as he had would have so little knowledge. He'd know most of what had happened and all about those he worked with. And he was an expert with pheromones. It would have been easy for him to have arranged Hayter's death—maybe the price of Zucco's cooperation. And to have arranged the klachen's attack. Reiza's scarf was a deliberate plant to divert suspicion. He wanted me to concentrate on Zucco.''

''And all the time he was an agent of the Cyclan.'' Shakira finished his wine and said, ''They must want you very badly, Earl.''

''They do.''

''So I gathered. The cyber who came looking for you was most insistent. Cyber Tron—Valaban mentioned him.''

''You can find him at the Dubedat Hotel.'' Dumarest met the other's eyes, holding them as he rose from his chair. Around him the office took on a new quietness as if the very walls could sense the mounting tension. ''Are you thinking of selling me?''

''No, Earl!'' Shakira lifted his hands. ''No—I swear it!''

''Could you?''

''Elagonya no longer has power over you. I have kept to our bargain. Freedom from restraint, money,'' Shakira gestured to the bag lying on the desk, ''and fortunately you are not in need of medical attention. Only Melome is left.''

She rose as they entered her room, running forward to catch Dumarest by the hand, her face radiant with smiles.

''Earl! You came! I knew you would!''

''And you know why.''

''Yes.'' A shadow touched her face, gone as soon as born. ''Elagonya explained why you must do what you do and why I must not be a selfish child. To deny is not to love, Earl, and I love you.''

''In your fashion, Melome.''

''Yes,'' she agreed. ''In my fashion as you love me in yours. Shall we begin?''

He sat and she took her place facing him, also cross-legged so they resembled two idols set as a pair on some ancient altar. Then she stirred, extending her hands for Dumarest to take.

As he closed his fingers around them he said, ''You know what I need, Melome, please help me to find it. Send me back to that time in the past when I knew terror. The fear of discovery when I was in the captain's cabin. I must go back to that time. I must!''

To see the open book, to read it, to gain the coordinates of Earth!

To put an end to the long and painful search.

Music flowed from the recorder as Shakira touched a control, the air filling with the wail of pipes and the sonorous beat of a drum. Dumarest felt the hands he held grow chill as if the girl was withdrawing all but essential energy in order to power her song. One which came as it had come before, filling his mind, the room, the universe with its dominating cadences.

And again he was thrown on a mental journey back through time.

To feel again the stomach-gripping fear, the chill, the pain of terror.

A wind thick with knives and a sky blotched by the baleful eyes of a single moon. Snow on the ground and ice rimming the pond. A night in which too many would die and he knew that he would be one of them.

The blanket he wore was torn, thin, crusted with dirt. More dirt masked his face and rimmed his mouth, the coating marked with paths of mucous from his nostrils, wind-born tears from his eyes. A child, begging, knowing that charity was dead. To steal was his only hope of survival. To be caught was to know pain.

And he had been caught.

The hand which gripped his wrist forced it closer to the fire, the pot smoking above it. A container half-full of seething stew, thin, odorous, but containing the nourishment he had to have.

"A thief," said the man holding him. "Caught him reaching for the pot. Guess he thought I was asleep."

"His bad luck you weren't." The other's voice was thick with drowsiness. "He get anything?"

"No."

"Good. We won't have to slice off a foot so as to make it up. Just teach him a lesson and let him go."

Harsh times and harsh justice and the lesson wouldn't be easy to take. The terror mounted as his hand was forced closer to the fire, closer until he felt the burning kiss of flame, the searing of his skin, the agony which flowed from the spot.

One small against the possibility of what could happen if his captor chose.

A finger burned to the bone. A hand burned to the wrist.

"God! God! God, please God! Make him let me go!"

Then his free hand dipping, plunging into the soup, lifting from the seething liquid to splash the near-boiling wetness into his captor's face. Freedom as the man cried out and then the running, the hiding, the plunging of burned hands into the snow. The luck as a rodent, startled by his action, crashed from hiding to land against his chest.

"No," said Dumarest. "No."

"Earl?" Melome's face was a blur before him. "Do you want to stop?"

"The wrong time. Too early." Dumarest heard his voice, thick, mumbling. "Try again. Later. Later."

"You should rest." Shakira's voice held a genuine concern. "Take a glass of wine."

Sit and talk and waste the time that was left. To squander the precious minutes and lose the chance of learning what he had to know.

"Keep going."

"But—"

"Do it!" A burned hand, a night of fear and terror which had happened long ago. A thing he could live with and already it was fading. "Try again, Melome. Again."

And the pipe, the drum, the wailing song with its soaring cadences which held a rare and unusual magic. One which worked as he listened. As the girl changed, the room in which he sat.

One to turn into the round dial of an instrument set against a wall. The other into a cabin.

Dumarest felt his stomach churn as he listened to the sound of approaching footsteps.

They would find him and take him before the captain and he would be punished as they had said others had been. Taken and flogged until his bones showed through the lacerated flesh or sealed in a suit and evicted into space with an hour's air. Or put into the generator where invisible energies would rot his bones and send him blind and turn him into a thing of horror.

Threats whispered in idle hours. Tales of torments done and stories woven from sick minds and fevered imaginations. The fruit of loneliness and frustration to be showered on an ignorant boy.

He turned, seeking employment for his hands, a visible task to justify his presence in the cabin. An added defense should anyone look in. A duster was to hand and he used it, nearing the table, the book resting on it. A fat volume, the pages open, sheets bearing rows of the captain's script.

Dumarest looked at it as he plied the duster. Hearing the

footsteps outside the cabin fade into silence. Seeing the pages thin and vanish as the moment of terror ebbed away.

"Success," said Shakira. "There is nothing so satisfying. Come, Earl, let us drink to it."

The wine he served was rich and darkly red, the same as he'd produced before. Then it had reminded Dumarest of blood, now it held the acrid taste of defeat.

"It was success, Earl?" The circus owner's voice sharpened as he saw Dumarest's unfinished wine. "Melome said you had returned to the right time. She was sure of it."

"She was right."

"Then—"

"You want to share my knowledge. The bargain we made." Dumarest reached for a sheet of paper. "I went back and I saw the book. This is what I read."

He wrote and passed the sheet to Shakira who picked it up and held it before his eyes.

"The cargo we loaded on Ascanio was spoiled and had to be unloaded at a total loss," he murmured, reading. "A bad trip with no prospect of improvement so I took a chance and risked a journey to the proscribed planet. A waste of time—the place is a nightmare. God help the poor devils who lived here. Those remaining are degenerate scum little more than savage animals. Found a stowaway after we'd left, a boy who looks human. He claims to be twelve but looks younger and could be dangerous. Decided to take a chance and kept him but if he shows any sign of trouble I'll have to—"

Shakira looked at Dumarest. "Is this all?"

"Yes."

"But you were so sure there would be more."

"I was wrong." Dumarest gulped at his wine. "The book was a journal, not the ship's log. A private diary of events. And I could only look at it. I couldn't turn the pages. The coordinates could have been written plain on the previous sheet but I'll never know. Not even if I went back could I ever know."

"And you can't go back. Terror, relived, loses its impact. You could try for a dozen years and never again hit that exact period. But it lives in your mind. Your memory. Perhaps—"

"The facts remain," said Dumarest. He was curt. "I saw the book, remembered what it said, wrote it down. You have it in your hand. All of it. Useless rubbish!"

Words for which he had risked his life. Once they had him in their power the Cyclan would not be gentle. They would sear his brain with electric probes, test him with endless pain, tear him apart cell by cell in order to regain their lost secret. And time was running out.

"Wait!" Shakira lifted a hand as Dumarest rose to his feet. "Disappointment has blunted your natural shrewdness. The coordinates are lacking, true, but still you have won information. The name of a world, Ascanio. It must be relatively close to the proscribed planet. Earth? But why should it be proscribed? And by whom? And the rest? That about the boy who was found—you?"

"It has to be."

"A strange description. Malnutrition would account for your size, but why should he think you dangerous? Sit, my friend, take some more wine, let us consider this. You may have gained more than you realize."

Shakira brooded over the paper as Dumarest followed his suggestion. A few more minutes against what the other's fresh viewpoint could gain. Extra danger set against the possibility of winning gold from apparent dross.

"Proscribed," murmured Shakira. "Set apart. Outlawed. Banned. Incredible that a world should be so treated. But by whom? And how to enforce the proscription?"

Questions which hung in the air as he considered the matter. A silence broken by an imperious knocking at the door.

"Who is it?" Shakira's tone held anger though his face remained as placid as before. "I gave orders that on no account should I be disturbed." The paper fell to the table as the knocking was repeated. "Who is there?"

The answer stepped through the opened panel, tall, thin, glowing in a scarlet robe. One adorned with the Seal of the Cyclan.

"Cyber Tron." Pushed Shakira had fallen back to the support of the table. Now he stood, hands lifted, facing the intruder. "What do you want here?"

"You know the answer to that." Tron lifted his hand, the gun it held. One like that used by Valaban. "Do not waste time calling for help. Those you set on guard have been taken care of." The guard moved to point at Dumarest, the wide orifice aimed directly at his face. "You are to come with me. Unless you obey me implicitly I shall fire. The shot will not kill you but

156

your face will be ruined, your eyes. Even in the open a blind man cannot get far."

And in the maze of the circus it would be impossible. Dumarest froze where he sat, hands on the table, one close to the glass holding his wine. Across the board Shakira faced the cyber, hands still lifted in his pathetic gesture of appeal or surrender. An act? One to cover his betrayal? The face remained a mask and gave no hint as to the answer.

Dumarest said, "It seems you win, Cyber Tron. But I expected you earlier. What delayed you?"

"You will not move and you will not talk." Tron's face, like Shakira's, did not change expression but his eyes revealed his pleasure. "Disobey and I fire."

A good moment and he relished it; the prediction had been correct. Now, even though the agent had failed, Dumarest was held fast in the trap. One now sealed tight by his own presence.

"You will lift both hands and place them on your head," said Tron. "You will make no other movement." Then, as Dumarest made no move to obey, "Do it or—"

"You will fire. I know. You told me." Dumarest saw the tightening of the finger on the trigger and added, quickly, "To shoot me would be proof of your inefficiency. A blind man needs help—who will give it? Can you trust them? Could you watch them? It would be far more logical to keep me functional." Dumarest moved a finger closer to the glass of wine. A poor weapon but the only one available. "There is always the possibility of error should you fire. How can you be certain as to the charge? The damage it could do? And what of the trauma of the wound?"

Arguments to ease the tension and so lessen the immediate danger, but ones which he knew weren't going to work. Tron was too determined. Dumarest looked at the gun, knowing that before he could move it would fire. That it was only a matter of seconds before it did.

"Efficiency is a matter of adjusting action to the relevant situation," said Tron. "Your points are valid but negated by the paramount need to ensure your captivity. Therefore—"

Shakira screamed.

It was a sound like grating metal, a nail dragged over a slate, loud, shocking, totally unexpected. As the cyber turned toward him Shakira stepped forward, hands high, voice pleading.

"No! Don't! Please don't! I beg you not to do it!"

Words which masked action, even as he spoke the fabric of his blouse ripped open from neck to waist to reveal a hand. Holding a gun.

A laser which fired as Dumarest snatched up the glass and threw it as Tron fired at the same time. A blast which tore at Shakira's face and sent him turning as the cyber fell with smoke pluming from the ruined pattern of his insignia.

"Shakira!" Dumarest rose from his examination of the dead man. "How badly are you hurt?" He had tried to divert Tron's aim but knew he had failed. "Shakira?"

The owner remained turned away, hands to his face, leaning against the edge of the table. Something cracked beneath Dumarest's foot as he stepped toward him and he looked at the fragment beneath his boot. One of several lying scattered around; scraps of flesh-coloured plastic holding a limited flexibility.

Dumarest knew what they had to be.

"A mask," he said. "You wear a mask."

One shattered and ruined by the blast from the cyber's gun, but what other damage had been done? Shakira turned away as Dumarest reached him.

"Please. The mask is damaged, true, but I have another. In the bottom drawer of my desk. Be so good as to face the wall while I don it."

"I'll do that." Dumarest reached again for the shielding hands. "But only after I've seen what injuries you have."

A moment and they were exposed, ugly welts scored on flesh but harmless enough. The mask had taken the brunt of the shot, shattering like an eggshell but saving the wearer. One now revealed for what he was.

"You are disgusted," said Shakira. "I can read it in your eyes."

"No. You see what you expect to find. I'm concerned, not disgusted." Then, as the other made no comment, Dumarest added in a burst of sudden anger, "What kind of a man do you take me for? You saved my life—what the hell do I care what you look like?"

"You are kind. The other mask?"

"You don't need it."

"For you, no, but for others? And I must maintain the habit of wearing it. Help yourself to wine, Earl. I shall not be long."

It still held the color of blood and the acrid taste of defeat, but now a new dimension had been added, one of alien scope.

Dumarest sat, drinking, remembering how Shakira had looked when the last of the ruined mask had been discarded. The bald, rounded head, the protruding eyes, the noseless face, the mouth, the jaw—against him Elagonya was beautiful.

But there had been more than a distortion of the familiar, the visage had held inhuman facets as had the eyes as if an alien form of life had been so disfigured as to ape the human frame.

"Pour me wine, Earl." Shakira had returned, his face seemingly as it had been, but more stiff now as if the mask were an earlier model, made before he had recognized the necessity of falsifying a smile. "Thank you." He drank and set down his glass. "We each have secrets, Earl. Do we agree never to divulge them?"

"Of course." Dumarest looked at the dead cyber. "And him?"

"He will be disposed of."

"In the sump?" Dumarest guessed the answer. "He will be missed and others will come after him."

"When they do I shall tell them of the tragic accident which took so many lives. Valaban's, the cyber's, yours." Shakira picked up his glass and took a sip of wine. "A good story, my friend, and there will be those to swear to its truth. And they will not lie."

Primed and conditioned by the sensitives Shakira controlled. The powers he owned which could delude the test of machines. Dumarest relaxed even as he wondered why Shakira should go to so much trouble. He had been made a part of the circus and the circus took care of its own, but was that the real answer?

"More wine?" Shakira poured and sipped his own. "We have much in common, Earl, you and I. When I was very young I never guessed how different to others I was. My family was wealthy and kept me apart. I grew up attended by those I thought normal. It was only later, when I left home, I realized what a hell the universe could be."

He made the familiar gesture, hands lifting to hover as if in appeal or surrender, but now Dumarest knew it to be neither. The lifting of the hands and arms was to give clearance to the other hands hidden beneath the blouse. The armless appendages sprouting from the waist like vestigial limbs.

"But I found a solution."

"You bought the circus."

"More than that, Earl, I bought a home." Shakira sipped

again at his wine, his voice softened with memories. "The circus of Chen Wei," he said. "Once the name meant Golden Joy, or so I was told but Chen Wei could have lied. He often did. But for me the name was no lie. I had found the one place where I could be accepted for what I was. A haven against all those who despise the unusual and who want to hunt down and destroy the different. And I could do more. I could provide a home for others like Elagonya and Melome and even you, Earl. But the circus is not for you.

"And yet you could find happiness here. Melome loves you."

"She is still young."

"And you love something more. Your hunt. Your search for home. And I think I can help you to find it. Here." Shakira reached for paper and wrote on it, folding it before handing it to Dumarest. "A name and a world, Earl. One not too distant. The man is unusual and if anyone can help you he can. Go to him. Tell him I sent you. Tell him what you know."

Dumarest said, "Why are you doing this for me?"

"You saved my circus for me from Zucco. My home, Earl, my world. Can I do less for you?" Shakira lifted his glass. "A toast, my friend. To your success!" Then, as the glasses were lowered, he said with a sudden, raw urgency, "Find your world, Earl. Find Earth. And find it soon—we freaks must have somewhere to call our own!"